NO SAFE PLACE

Pandemic Book Three

CHRISTINE KERSEY

SAPPHIRE
CREEK
PRESS

The characters and events portrayed in this book are fictitious. Any similarity to real persons, living or dead, is coincidental and not intended by the author.

No Safe Place (Pandemic Book Three)

Copyright © 2019 by Christine Kersey

Cover by Novak Illustration

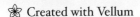 Created with Vellum

BOOKS BY CHRISTINE KERSEY

EMP COLLAPSE

Chaos Begins (EMP Collapse Book One)

Pandemic

Pandemic: The Beginning (Pandemic Book One)

Forced Exodus (Pandemic Book Two)

No Safe Place (Pandemic Book Three)

Insurrection (Pandemic Book Four)

Parallel World

Dare to Resist (Parallel World Book One)

Dare to Endure (Parallel World Book Two)

Dare to Defy (Parallel World Book Three)

Dare to Oppose (Parallel World Book Four)

Dare to Prevail (Parallel World Book Five)

Witness Series

Witness (Witness, Book 1)

Retribution (Witness, Book 2)

Billionaires Find Love

The Protective Billionaire

The Missing Billionaire

The Secret Billionaire

The Billionaire Handyman

Last First Kiss Romance Series

Never Kiss Your Bodyguard

Never Kiss Your Fake Fiancé

Emerald Falls Romance Series

Crushing On You (Emerald Falls, Book One)

Dangerous Lies (Emerald Falls, Book Two)

Chance Encounter (Emerald Falls, Book Three)

Her Billionaire Ex-Boyfriend Fake Fiancé (Christmas in Emerald Falls)

Fair Catch Romance

Protected by the Quarterback

False Start

Blindsided

Pass Interference

Pass Protection

Game On

Ashley's Billionaire

Snowed in with the Billionaire

Assistant to the Billionaire

Trouble with the Billionaire

Ever After with the Billionaire

Park City Firefighter Romance

Rescue My Heart

Hearts On Fire

Searching for Love

Falling for You (Searching for Love, Book One)

Finding Reese (Searching for Love, Book Two)

Surrender My Heart (Searching for Love, Book Three)

Bring Me Home (Searching for Love, Book Four)

Lily's Story

He Loves Me Not (Lily's Story, Book 1)

Don't Look Back (Lily's Story, Book 2)

Love At Last (Lily's Story, Book 3)

Life Imperfect (Lily's Story, Book 4)

Over You Series

Over You

Second Chances (sequel to Over You)

Standalone Suspense

Suspicions

No Way Out

CHAPTER ONE

Jessica

"THANK YOU," Jessica said as she accepted a thick slice of freshly baked bread from Sarah Miller. The lovely scent wafted into her nose, making her salivate, but she forced herself to wait until everyone had been served. Even in the apocalypse she could have good manners. A smile tilted her lips at the thought.

She looked at the others in her group—her husband Matt and their kids, Dylan, Kayla and Brooke. Then there was Jeff and Emily, Derrick, Chris and Amy and their two boys, and Paisley and her daughter Serena. They'd only arrived at Frank and Sarah Miller's house half an hour earlier, but already she felt an overwhelming sense of peace. This place could really become home—if Emily's aunt and uncle allowed them to stay. Which Jessica was determined to make happen. She had to. They'd been through hell over the last forty-eight hours and she wanted to shield her children from all the ugliness that this new world had foisted upon them. If that was even possible.

How far would she go to make that happen? Three weeks earlier, before the bird flu had killed ninety-five percent of the world's population, if someone had told her she would shoot a stranger in the foot in the women's room at a rest stop, she would have thought they'd gone completely insane. Yet that was exactly what had happened just the day before.

Was that woman still alive? The woman had said she was all alone since Jessica's group had killed the two men she'd been traveling with. Guilt and sorrow pierced Jessica. Yet, she would do it all over again to protect her daughter. With a sudden clarity that shook her to the core, she knew that she would do *anything* to protect her family. Even kill.

She didn't want to do that, not at all. But she would.

"Aren't you going to eat?" Matt asked from beside her, and she realized she'd been staring off into space, lost in thought.

Shaking off the dark thoughts, she lifted the bread from the plate with a smile. "Definitely." She held the bread to her nose and inhaled the heavenly scent before taking a small bite. She wanted to savor every morsel.

"Mmmm," Brooke murmured from where she sat cross-legged on the concrete patio as she ate her slice. Cleo, Brooke's German shepherd, lay at her feet, her chin resting on her paws in contentment. Jessica smiled at Brooke. She wasn't her daughter by birth, but when both of Brooke's parents had died from the bird flu, she and Matt had taken her in as their own. And they would protect her as their own too.

"This is delicious, Aunt Sarah," Emily said with a smile. "Thank you."

Everyone nodded in agreement.

A look of regret swept over Sarah's face. "I'm afraid I won't be able to bake many more loaves. I'm almost out of flour."

"We'll get you more," Jeff, Emily's boyfriend, said. He was sitting on the patio, his long legs stretched out in front of him.

Sarah looked at him with raised eyebrows. "Really? And how are you going to do that?"

Jeff chuckled. "There's gotta be plenty of places we can scavenge."

Frank, Sarah's husband, made a scoffing sound. "Only if the Emperors haven't already taken it."

Just the mention of the gang who had robbed them of almost everything they had that very day sent a wave of anger and terror cascading over Jessica. She heard grumbles coming from the others and knew they all felt the same.

"I'm sure we can find something," Emily said.

What if they couldn't? Jessica and her group included fourteen people, most of them adults or teenagers. They would need a lot of food. If they couldn't provide for themselves, Frank and Sarah wouldn't allow them to stay. Where would she and her family go then? It was a dangerous world out there. She had to do whatever she could to keep her family safe.

Without thinking, she leapt to her feet. "Let's get started."

All eyes swiveled in her direction.

"Mom," Kayla said with a note of confusion, "we just got here. We're tired."

Many heads nodded in agreement. Feeling like she'd over-reacted to her own thoughts, Jessica sank back to her seat. Matt slid his hand into hers and gave her a supportive squeeze.

"Jessica's right," Derrick said, which bolstered her. "We should go soon."

Jeff stood. "I'm ready."

Looking at the people she now considered family, Jessica smiled.

"I'd like to get my kids settled first," Amy said with a glance at her two young boys. Six-year-old Jacob was climbing on Chris's lap, while Aaron, who was nearly two, was slumped against Amy's shoulder, fast asleep.

"Sit down, Jeff," Sarah said as a smile blossomed on her lips. "We have enough food for a few days, at least."

Frank picked up the conversation. "Let's take the rest of today to get everyone settled." He glanced meaningfully at Chris and Amy's boys as well as at Serena, Paisley's two-year-old daughter, then he swept his gaze over the rest of the group. "You can get acquainted with the property. See how the place is set up. That kind of thing."

Jeff settled back onto the ground beside Emily and

mumbled, "I just want my trailer back." Emily rested her hand on his arm. He glanced at her with a frown.

Jessica knew how he felt. If she and Matt had their RV, she and Matt and the kids could sleep in it. They'd be self-sufficient instead of relying on Frank and Sarah's kind hospitality. But it was gone. For good. She had to accept that. But it made her furious.

At least after the Emperors had robbed them blind, they'd let them go without hurting anyone. Randy, their leader, had flat-out said he would let them keep their RV and truck if Jessica and Matt let him have one of their daughters. The suggestion had been disgusting, the memory making Jessica's stomach churn with fear and loathing.

Thankfully, Randy had no idea that she and her family and friends were still in the area. With any luck, they'd never see any of the Emperors again. On the other hand, it was less than ten miles north of the Miller's farm that they'd had their run-in with the gang, so it was a distinct possibility that they would cross paths with Randy or one of his minions eventually.

Jessica desperately hoped that wouldn't happen.

"What did you have in your trailer?" Frank asked Jeff, pulling Jessica out of her thoughts.

Frowning deeply, Jeff shook his head. "Food, and lots of it. Two tents, four sleeping bags, as well as other camping gear." His jaw clenched. "And all of my guns." This last bit he said in a near growl.

"We still have guns," Chris said with a smirk. "All of the confiscated guns."

Frank's eyebrows shot up. "Confiscated guns? What are you talking about?"

Matt recounted what had happened at the inspection station earlier that day. Half-listening, all Jessica could think about was the way that man who worked for the government had slammed Matt's face into the hood of his truck, breaking his nose. It had been absolutely awful and Jessica had felt completely helpless.

She glanced at Matt, taking in his swollen nose and the bruising around his eyes. It had to be painful but Matt hadn't complained once.

She and Matt and their family had been at the mercy of those men who had wanted to take every one of their guns in the name of the Governor of California. Maybe Matt shouldn't have resisted, but Jessica was proud that he had.

It would have been a lot worse if Jeff hadn't shown up when he had, shooting the leader of the group point blank. Jeff was definitely an asset to their group. Ex-military, as were Derrick and Chris, he wasn't afraid to confront bullies. Seemed to relish it, actually.

"Let me take a look at that nose," Sarah said to Matt.

Jessica remembered that Emily had said her aunt was a nurse. She watched as Sarah examined Matt's nose before inviting him into the house. A short time later he came back, sporting a bandage across the bridge of his nose.

"Feeling better?" Jessica asked him as he sat beside her.

Half-smiling, he nodded. "As good as anyone can feel after having their nose broken."

She kissed him on the cheek. "At least it won't be crooked. Right?"

His shoulders lifted in a shrug. "Hope not. Wouldn't want to mar this handsome face."

Jessica laughed, then heard others chuckling. She looked at those around her. Warmth spread throughout her chest. This was her tribe, her family.

Frank stood. "Let me give you the tour."

CHAPTER TWO

Matt

"We have enough room to plant a much larger garden," Frank said. "Just need more seeds."

Matt looked over the plot of land growing a wide array of vegetables and thought about the seeds he'd picked up for Jessica at the Home Depot back home. They, along with so many other valuable things, had been taken when Randy had stolen their RV. Feeling that familiar rage beginning to billow inside him, he had to work to suppress it and focus on what he did have. Namely, his family. That was the most important thing. Anyway, maybe they could find some seeds when they went out scavenging.

"It's a beautiful garden," Paisley said. "And so nice that you can plant early here. In Idaho we have to wait until May."

Matt studied Paisley. They'd picked her and her daughter up from the side of the road the day before. He remembered her saying she'd grown up on a farm. Which would make her a lot more useful than he would be. Humbled by the thought, he looked at the rows of carrots, tomato, corn, cucumbers, and other vegetables, grateful that they'd landed someplace safe.

Frank nodded. "We planted in late March. Just a few weeks ago." He shook his head. "Seems like another lifetime now."

In late March the flu wasn't on Matt's radar. But now? Now, it had turned his life upside down.

"That small orchard," Frank said, pointing to two rows of leafy trees, "has a variety of fruit trees. We've got plums, nectarines, apples, cherries. And of course," he added, pointing to orchards that bordered his property on three sides, "almond trees are everywhere."

What a bounty! Matt was kind of astonished as he looked at the sustenance growing in every direction. So much more grew here than at home in Utah. When Emily had said that the San Joaquin Valley was rich with agriculture, she hadn't been exaggerating. Despite the bad elements like the Emperors, it was still a wonderful place to be.

Next, Frank showed them his spacious barn, which held a variety of equipment, including a tractor, then they walked over to the pasture where a small herd of cows as well as four horses grazed. A large chicken coop with a number of chickens sat nearby. Frank pointed out the San Joaquin River, which flowed behind the property. A short path led to a small dock.

"Good source of water," Derrick said.

"Only if we get desperate," Frank said.

Matt turned to Frank. "You have another source?"

A wide grin split Frank's face. "We're on well water here."

"Wait. Don't you need electricity to pump the well?"

"Sure do. Which is why I'm glad I let Sarah talk me into getting a solar well pump."

"He didn't want to get it," Sarah said. "Complained about the cost like no other, but I insisted." She smiled at him. "For once, he listened."

Frank chuckled. "Like I said, glad I did." Then he frowned. "Just wish I'd listened and gotten solar for the rest of the house."

Sarah shook her head like she'd already given him the "I told you so" speech and didn't want to do it again.

"That's okay, Uncle Frank," Emily said with a smile. "Having water is huge. Plus, with septic for sewer and propane for the stove and water heater, we're in great shape."

Matt agreed. Running water and flushing toilets and hot showers would be amazing, but he couldn't help but worry that someone would want to take it all away from them. What if the Emperors found out what they had? Would they steal it from them? Force them out? After the neighborhood cooperative had burned his house down, Matt knew that people would do whatever they had to to get what they wanted. Especially with no one to enforce law and order.

"What do you think?" Jessica whispered beside him, her eyes lighting with hope. "Isn't this place wonderful?"

It was. But would it be better to go somewhere else and get used to living with less rather than getting comfortable here and having it taken away? Swallowing down his worry, he forced a smile. "Yeah."

Jessica's eyebrows tugged together like she knew he was keeping his true feelings from her, but he just smiled brighter.

"What's that?" Amy asked, pointing to what looked like a playhouse. A sign that read *Garden* hung from the eaves.

"That's the well house," Frank said. "There's some gardening equipment in there too, but I built it to house the well for the water."

Feeling a mix of elation and worry, Matt nodded.

"Okay," Sarah said with one eyebrow arched, "let's go inside and see if we can figure out where everyone will sleep."

This was the part that would be harder to make work for their numbers. There was no way Frank and Sarah could comfortably fit all of them inside long-term. They would have to come up with another solution.

"Come on in," Sarah said as she led them onto the wide back porch and through the patio door.

They shuffled though the open door, then gathered in the spacious living room. Once everyone was inside, Frank looked at Sarah. A gentle smile curved her lips as she said, "We were never able to have children, so Emily is like a daughter to us."

Emily walked over to Sarah and gave her a hug. "Thank you, Aunt Sarah."

Sarah nodded, then slid her gaze over the assembled group.

"We have two spare bedrooms on the main floor, and a bonus space above the garage where we can put an air mattress." She chuckled. "That used to be more than enough space, but now?" One of her eyebrows quirked up. "Now, it will be a challenge." She glanced at Frank, who nodded. "Frank and I have the master bedroom, of course, but the other three rooms, well, I think the couples should each have a private room. The rest can sleep in here." She swept her arms outward, encompassing the living room as well as a small office that was adjacent to the living room.

That sounded great to Matt, and when he looked at the others, they were nodding or smiling like they agreed. At this point they were all just very appreciative that Frank and Sarah were letting them stay at all.

"Thank you for your hospitality," Matt said. "We're truly grateful."

"Agreed," Derrick said.

"Maybe down the road," Frank said, "we can create some additional housing."

That brought a lift to Matt's eyebrows. Was Frank implying he would let them stay?

"If," he added, his voice stern, "having you all here works out."

Okay. So, it was still uncertain, although Matt believed the idea was growing on Frank. Matt would do everything he could to prove that having them there was an asset rather than a burden

"Let me show you the rooms," Sarah said to Matt, Jessica,

Chris, and Amy. She smiled at Jeff and Emily. "You'll use your usual room."

The two couples followed Sarah down the hall where two bedrooms were situated with a bathroom in between. "This room is where Jeff and Emily always stay. The four of you can decide who gets the other bedroom down here and who gets the space over the garage."

Beyond thrilled that he and Jessica would have a private room, Matt didn't care which room was theirs.

Amy glanced at Matt and Jessica. "If it's all the same to you, I'd like to stay on the main floor so we're close to where our boys are sleeping."

Matt glanced at Jessica, who nodded, then said, "Works for us."

"Let me show you where you'll sleep," Sarah said.

Matt and Jessica followed her through the living room and kitchen and down a short hallway. At the end, on the left, was a door that led to the garage, while on the right was a staircase. Up the stairs they went, and when they reached the top, he saw a landing with two doors—one led to a spacious open area and the other to a small bathroom.

This place was getting better and better. Paradise, as far as he was concerned. He turned to Sarah. "This is amazing."

She smiled at him. "Despite Frank's grumpiness, we're glad you're here. We've been worried about the Emperors and…" Her eyes tightened with concern as she shook her head. "Now though, I feel much safer."

Warmth for Emily's aunt shot through Matt. He smiled.

"We'll do everything we can to protect this place." The farm was a safe haven from this brutal world and Matt had every intention of keeping it that way.

That night, as Matt and Jessica snuggled in the sleeping bags they'd zipped together, he relished the sense of security being in this house gave him.

Until a knock sounded on his door.

"Come in."

Jeff poked his head in. "Both of you get up. Someone's here." Then he closed the door.

Alarmed, Matt turned to Jessica. Her eyes were wide.

CHAPTER THREE

Jessica

JESSICA WONDERED who it could be. The Emperors? A different enemy? Certainly no one friendly. Not this late at night. It was past ten o'clock.

She climbed out of the sleeping bag and yanked on a pair of jeans and a t-shirt by the light of the moon trickling in through the open blinds. Matt had already thrown on a pair of sweats and a t-shirt and was tying his shoes.

"Who do you think it is?" she asked, as if Matt knew something she didn't.

He shook his head. "No idea." Pausing briefly, he added, "I don't hear any shooting or yelling or anything, so maybe it's nothing bad."

She hoped he was right, but her heart stuttered with fear nonetheless. Then she remembered that their children were in the living room. Downstairs. Forgoing putting on her shoes, she hurried to their bedroom door and pulled it open. "The kids. We need to hurry."

Clearly understanding her intent, Matt was right behind her. They dashed to the top of the stairs, but when calm voices floated upward, Jessica's pounding heartbeat began to settle. She glanced at Matt, who looked just as confused as she felt, then she descended the stairs and made her way into the living room.

The space was lit with a variety of candles sitting on side tables and the entertainment center. A battery-powered lantern sat in the middle of the coffee table, illuminating the assembled group. All of the adults, along with the teenagers, were sitting or standing—the little ones were asleep in the adjacent office space. In the center of it all sat a man who looked to be in his early seventies. He had a cane resting across his thighs. Frank and Sarah sat on either side of him on the couch talking to him in low voices.

"Everyone's here now," Jeff said with a look in Jessica and Matt's direction.

All eyes went to them before going back to the old man.

"Sit here, Mom," Dylan said, standing from the chair where he'd been sitting before settling on the floor nearby.

"Thanks, honey," Jessica said as she sat in the vacated chair while Matt leaned against a wall.

"Sorry to wake you," Frank began, his gaze gliding over the group. He looked at the visitor. "This is Walter Powell. He lives down the road."

Her eyes riveted on the man, Jessica waited to see what

was so important that the entire group needed to gather together after they'd already gone to bed.

Walter cast his gaze around, seeming to take the measure of each and every one of them, then he looked at Frank and gave him a grim smile. He adjusted his cane across his lap. "Frank told me you all just arrived here today."

Heads nodded all around.

"He also told me that you had an encounter with the Emperors."

At the mention of the gang who'd terrorized them and stolen all they had, Jessica felt her chest tighten with a mix of fear and anger.

"That's right," Jeff said in a tone that showed he was still furious that his truck and trailer had been taken. "What do you know about them?"

Eyes narrowing, Walter focused on Jeff. "I remember you." He glanced at Emily. "Have you married Frank and Sarah's niece yet?"

Jeff's jaw tightened but he didn't reply.

Walter made a scoffing sound. "Didn't think so."

"Why are you here?" Derrick asked, obviously trying to refocus the conversation to what was most important.

Walter looked his way. "We need to unite."

Uniting reminded Jessica of the neighborhood cooperative back home, which was why they'd had to flee in the first place. She looked at Matt. His eyebrows had shot up as he stared at Walter. It looked like he felt the same way she did.

"What did you have in mind?" Derrick asked, evidently willing to listen before shutting the man down.

"We have a common enemy in the Emperors," Walter started. "If we band together we'll be able to fight them, to keep them from taking all we have."

Jessica couldn't help but think that uniting would only benefit Walter. After all, their group had several battle-hardened members. Who did Walter have? Besides, she didn't want to be in a war. Especially when the Emperors had no idea that she and the rest of her group were still around. She would prefer to fly under the radar and keep their presence quiet.

"What have they taken from you?" Jeff asked.

Lips pursing, Walter wrapped his hands around his cane until his knuckles turned white, then, with jaw clenched, he said, "Everything that matters."

What did that mean? Jessica had to know more. "Can you be more specific?"

All eyes shifted to her before boomeranging back to Walter. He cleared his throat like he was getting his emotions under control. "I lost my wife well before the bird flu hit, but that nasty flu took my daughter. Her husband and three children were spared." His chin quivered, which surprised Jessica. Then he lifted his chin and stared into the distance. "My grandchildren—all that's left of my daughter, you understand..." He shook his head and briefly closed his eyes before blinking and sweeping his gaze across the group. "Three nights ago, those Emperors took two of them—both of the teenagers."

Gasps filled the room, including Jessica's. And when she remembered the way Emperor Randy had licked his lips while suggesting keeping either Kayla or Brooke, she couldn't stop a shudder from cascading through her body.

"Boys or girls?" Derrick asked. "Your grandchildren they took."

"One of each," Walter said in a near-whisper. "My other grandson—he's only seven—is home with my son-in-law."

Knowing that Randy had Walter's grandchildren made Jessica sick. What had he done with them? Were they suffering? Were they even still alive?

Her first instinct was to help Walter get his grandchildren back, but before the thought could fully form in her mind, she pictured Randy's face, saw the tattoos snaking up both of his arms, remembered the evil that poured off of him like poison. The fear of confronting him hit her like a physical thing and she actually recoiled. She didn't want to be anywhere near him. She didn't want anyone she cared about to be anywhere near him either.

Had coming to this place been a mistake? Had she and Matt put their children in grave danger?

She sought out Matt with her eyes, and when he looked at her, she saw her worry reflected there.

CHAPTER FOUR

Matt

ON THE SURFACE, Walter's suggestion made sense to Matt. Join forces to fight the bad guys. But who was on Walter's side? Had he recruited others? Or were Matt and his group the first ones he'd gone to? The only ones who would do the fighting?

Matt could see in Jessica's face the concern that he felt. He remembered looking into Randy's eyes and seeing nothing, like Randy had no soul. The man was evil incarnate. Matt didn't want to tangle with him. Not unless he had to. There had been at least a dozen Emperors with Randy when Matt and his family had been forced off the freeway. How many more were there?

This was nothing like facing the neighborhood cooperative back home. This was ten times worse.

Overwhelmed, all Matt knew was that he had no desire to come into contact with Randy or his gang ever again.

"I have some questions," Chris said.

Matt looked at Chris and his wife Amy. Their two young boys were sound asleep on the floor of the small study nearby. How would it be to have such a young family to protect? Then he looked at his own family. Two beautiful teenaged daughters and a fourteen-year-old son. They were vulnerable too. Probably more vulnerable than Chris's kids. Anyway he sliced it, this was all bad.

"What are your questions?" Walter asked, his voice steady now.

"How many people have you recruited?"

Matt was glad Chris was asking the question he was sure they were all wondering.

Walter shook his head. "Only a few so far. But we'll get more. I'm sure of it."

For a full minute, no one spoke, no one volunteered to join Walter in his crusade, and as the silence dragged on, Walter slowly rose, pressing the foot of his cane into the thick carpet as he leaned on it. "Okay then," he said with a sigh, "I'll let you talk it over and you can get back to me." He looked at Frank. "You know where to find me."

Frank nodded, then walked Walter to the door before coming back to the couch. The sound of a vehicle starting up filled the night, and as the sound of the engine faded, Matt turned to the group with a deep frown. "We've already fought bad people back home. That's why we drove seven hundred miles. To start fresh. Not to start a brand-new war."

"Walter is a good man," Frank said as he leaned forward on the couch. "His grandkids are all he has now. I can't imagine what he must be going through." He shook his head, the glow of the lantern lighting up the frown on his face. "Wondering if his grandkids are okay." He looked at Matt's kids. "They're about your age, I think."

Matt could see dread etched on the faces of Kayla, Brooke, and Dylan. It ate him up to see his kids like that. He looked right at them. "That's not going to happen to you."

Sixteen-year-old Kayla wrapped her arms around herself. "How do you know?"

"We're not gonna let it," Derrick said, his voice low, his tone confident.

Matt regarded Derrick, who sat ramrod straight, his shoulders back and his chin up. Then he looked at Jeff and Chris. Their faces were just as set, just as firm. All three were ex-military. A fierce smile lifted the corners of Matt's lips. If they were going to be safe with anyone, it was with this group.

"What do you think Walter expects from us?" Matt asked.

Derrick frowned. "To fight the Emperors and save his grandkids."

Everyone was quiet, lost in their own thoughts.

Matt refused to imagine what it would be like if his own kids were taken by the Emperors—the idea was too awful. Instead, he pictured their small group going up against the Emperors' large gang. It would be a bloodbath.

"I don't know about the rest of you," Matt said, "but I don't want to start a war with the Emperors." A war that could kill people he loved.

"As much as I'd love to take Randy down," Derrick said, "my priority is keeping all of you safe. Going up against Randy and the rest of the Emperors would be the exact opposite."

Glad Derrick felt the same way he did, Matt looked at each person before saying, "Are we in agreement? We're going to stay away from the Emperors?" He glanced at Frank. Maybe Frank wanted to join with his friend. Was Matt endangering his family's place here by refusing to throw in his lot with Walter?

"All in favor of standing down," Derrick said.

Nearly every hand went up. The only ones that didn't belonged to Frank and Sarah.

All eyes shifted to them.

"You want to join with him, Uncle Frank?" Emily asked.

Frank sighed. "What I want is for life to go back to how it was, but that's not going to happen. In its place, I want to do what's right, and what's right is helping my longtime friend get his grandkids back."

Hearing it stated like that sent a stab of guilt right into Matt's heart. If it was *his* kids that had been taken, he would be desperate to get help from anyone. Still, he wasn't ready to risk the life of his family for Frank's friend. When no one said anything, Frank shook his head, took Sarah by the hand, and left the room.

"I want to do what's right too," Matt said, "but not at the expense of my family and all of you."

"We all feel guilty," Chris said. "I know I do." He sighed. "If things were different, if we didn't have our families to protect, then yeah, I'd be all for going after those creeps. But the reality is, as far as the Emperors know, we're long gone. I'd rather them keep thinking that."

"Part of me wants to go after Randy," Jeff said with a scowl. "Badly."

Emily looked at him with raised eyebrows. "But?"

Jeff chuckled. "But nothing. I want to take that loser down. Hard." He sobered. "But I'll abide by the consensus of the group. Besides, it's inevitable that we'll run in to Randy eventually. We can deal with him then."

Matt knew he was right and he dreaded that day. "Until then," Matt said, "I'd like to live in peace. I don't want to go out looking for trouble."

"Agreed," Derrick said. "We *just* got here." One side of his mouth tugged up in a grin. "Let's not stir up trouble. Yet."

"Let's not stir it up at all," Jessica said. "Why can't we just mind our own business and focus on surviving?"

Matt saw the earnestness on Jessica's face and wanted to reassure her that they could do exactly that, but in the back of his mind he knew they'd have to face Randy and the Emperors at some point. Randy and his crew believed they controlled this area. But this area was where Matt and his family lived now. A confrontation was unavoidable, although Matt dearly hoped that day was a long time off.

"Thinking about Walter's grandkids with those guys makes me sick to my stomach," Jessica said, her forehead creased. "But thinking about losing any of you terrifies me." She shook her head and softly sighed. "I'm just not ready to take that risk." Her voice lowered. "Not yet anyway."

"Those guys scared me," Paisley said. "I'd..." she shook her head. "I agree with Jessica. Mind our own business and stay out of it."

Amy smiled at Paisley and put a reassuring hand on her arm.

"I disagree," Dylan said.

Surprised, Matt turned to his son. "About what?"

Dylan's jaw was set as his hands clenched into fists. "We should take Randy out. He's a bully and a thief. And if he took some kids?" He shook his head, his nostrils flaring. "We could be next." He looked at Matt. "Don't say it won't happen to us. You don't know that."

Matt couldn't argue with him because he was right. Matt had no idea what the future held. But he would do everything within his power to make sure his kids weren't taken, and if that included not stepping up to save someone else's kids, then that's what he would do. Even if his son thought less of him for making that choice.

Derrick stood. "Look. We're all tired. We can discuss this in the morning."

Dylan sighed, his shoulders slumping.

Matt would talk to Dylan in private, try to help him understand his own point of view. In the meantime, he knew they couldn't let their guard down. Not for a minute. Had anyone been on watch when Walter had arrived? Everyone was in the same room now, so clearly no one was on watch at that moment.

Matt looked at Derrick. "What are we doing about security? I mean, no one's on watch right now."

Frowning, Derrick nodded. "That's a failure on my part. We should always have someone on watch."

"It's not all on you," Jeff said. "We're all adults here." He glanced at the three teenagers and chuckled. "Well, most of us."

"I can handle myself," Dylan said, obviously offended by Jeff's implication that he and the girls weren't fully capable of doing what the adults could do.

"No doubt," Jeff said, "and you'll definitely get your turn to be on watch, but we need to be deliberate in the way we go about it."

Dylan nodded as a bleak smile curved his lips.

"I'll work up a schedule," Jeff began, "make sure we have good coverage night and day, yet still get enough rest."

"Sounds good," Matt said.

"For tonight," Jeff said, "let's take two-hour shifts."

"I'll go first," Chris said. "Now until one a.m."

Heads nodded all around. Matt offered to do the one to three shift and Derrick volunteered to take three to five.

"Works for me," Jeff grinned. "I like to get up early anyway, so I'll do five to seven. By then everyone will be up and we can figure out a more permanent perimeter security plan."

"What about me?" Dylan asked, not about to be overlooked.

Matt smiled at him. "You can be with me from one to three." That would give him a chance to talk with him in private as well.

Dylan grinned. "Okay."

With that, everyone headed off to bed.

CHAPTER FIVE

Matt

"TIME TO GET UP," Matt said a few minutes before one as he gently shook Dylan's shoulder.

To Matt's surprise, once Dylan opened his eyes, he practically leapt out of his sleeping bag. "Okay. I just need to put my shoes on."

Chuckling, Matt said, "I don't remember you ever being so eager to get up for school."

Grinning, Dylan tugged on one shoe and began tying the laces. "This is nothing like school."

No, sadly, it wasn't. This was all about keeping bad guys away. Bad guys that they knew were out there. Bad guys that Matt desperately hoped wouldn't show up anytime soon.

"Ready," Dylan said as he stood next to Matt.

Matt looked at his son who was only a few inches shorter

than his own six feet. When had Dylan gotten so tall? "Okay. Let's head out."

Cleo stood from where she'd been curled up beside Brooke, stretching her back legs before walking toward them.

"Let's take Cleo with us," Matt said. He was always happy to have the help of the German shepherd when he was on watch. With her ability to hear someone approaching well before Matt could, she was an awesome early-warning system. "Let's go, girl," he whispered as he opened the front door and stepped onto the large porch.

He closed the door behind them and stopped, scanning the area. Cleo stood at attention beside him. The moon cast enough light for Matt to see across the manicured front lawn. The grass needed a trim, but Matt remembered Frank mentioning that he didn't want to waste gas running his lawn mower. Almond orchards surrounded the property on three sides, obscuring the drive that led out to the main road. Matt thought about when they'd arrived. The house hadn't been visible from the street. They'd had to drive down the road before it came into view. Perhaps the Emperors had no idea that the house was back here. The turnoff hadn't been obvious. That was a definite plus.

Cleo's tail thumped against Matt's leg, which was when he saw Chris striding toward them.

"Just did a perimeter check," Chris said. "Everything's quiet so far."

Nodding, Matt said, "Good to hear."

Chris reached out and gave Cleo a scratch between her ears, then straightened. "See you in the morning."

"'Night."

Continuing to survey the area within his view, Matt asked Dylan, "You armed?" Not that he wanted his son to have to use a gun. Ever. But he knew the reality. If his son wasn't prepared to defend himself, he would be vulnerable. Even so, Matt had every intention of keeping Dylan right by his side the entire shift.

"Yeah." Dylan's voice sounded more serious than Matt had heard it before. Good. He understood the gravity of the situation. Then again, Dylan had been there when the Emperors had held them at gunpoint. He'd seen all the terrible things they'd dealt with on the drive to California.

"Let me see your weapon."

Dylan handed it over.

Matt reviewed with him how to make sure a bullet was in the chamber and the safety was off, then handed the gun back to him. He did the same checks on his .45, then tucked it into his waist holster.

Matt descended the porch steps. Dylan and Cleo were right behind him.

As the trio walked the perimeter of Frank and Sarah's property, Matt thought about Dylan's eagerness to take Randy down. "Earlier you said you wanted to go after Randy." He kept his voice soft. In the silent darkness, every sound carried.

"Don't you?" Dylan's voice was incredulous. "I mean, he

took our truck and RV. I know you must be pissed about that."

"I am. No doubt about it. But those are just things. Objects that can be replaced. You and Mom and your sisters though..." He let the sentence trail off as sudden emotion clogged his throat. He swallowed over the knot. "People are what's important. Not things."

Dylan didn't speak for several beats. "I know. It's just..." He shook his head, his lips pursed in obvious anger. "It's just not right, what they did. Besides, Walter's grandkids are people."

That stung. Deeply. But only because it was true.

They passed the garden, the white buds on the tomato plants glowing in the moonlight.

"We live in a different world now, Dylan. The way people are? Their deepest, darkest desires? Those are going to be magnified. That's what happens when society breaks down, when the rules are gone and when people can get away with anything." Matt paused. "The world's become a very dark and ugly place."

Dylan nodded. "But we're not that way, right, Dad?"

A burst of warmth filled Matt's heart and he threw one arm over his son's shoulders as he tugged him in for a side-hug. "Nope. We're not that way." He released Dylan and they continued walking the property. Nothing moved as the stars shone above. It was difficult to see through the almond orchards, but from time to time Matt stopped and listened for intruders.

"I have a question."

Matt stopped and looked at Dylan. "What is it?"

Dylan gazed at Matt, his eyebrows furrowed. "If we want to make a difference, shouldn't we stand up for those who can't stand up for themselves?"

Matt's heart did a kind of ker-thump. Dylan was right. Completely right. But the thought of putting his family in danger terrified Matt. Still, what kind of example was he setting? Standing by and doing nothing while two kids were in mortal danger.

"You're talking about Walter's grandkids," Matt said, trying to buy himself time before he had to answer the actual question Dylan was asking.

"Yeah."

Slowly nodding, Matt began walking again as he scrambled to come up with a way to explain why he didn't want to get involved—he didn't know Walter and his family, he didn't want to risk the safety of his own family, he didn't want to reveal to the Emperors that Matt and his group were around. But each and every excuse was just that. An excuse to stay safe and sound at the farm as others suffered.

"You're right," he finally said. Dylan paused beside him, and when Matt looked at his son's face, he saw surprise. A smile played around the corners of Matt's lips, until he pictured Randy's dead eyes. "But even though you're right, unless our entire group is on board with tracking Randy and his gang down and doing something to stop them..." Matt shook his head, his mind racing with the horrible things that

35

could very well happen to Jessica, Kayla, Brooke, and Dylan if they did go after Randy.

"Dad? What were you going to say?"

Coming back to the here and now, Matt stopped and looked at Dylan. "This isn't something we can do alone. You saw how many people Randy had. And that was just the people that happened to be with him when they ambushed us. We have no idea how many people are in his gang or how ruthless they are." He shook his head.

Dylan's forehead creased like he hadn't considered how big a deal it would actually be.

Matt locked eyes with Dylan. "If we go after the Emperors —and that's still in question—we would have to be deliberate in how we do it. There would be a lot of planning and training involved." He exhaled softly. "We don't even know where they are."

"We can find them."

Not replying, Matt lifted his gaze and surveyed the farm, then he began walking. Dylan fell into step beside him.

"Can we look for them?" Dylan persisted.

Matt glanced at his son before going back to scanning everything within view. "Tell you what. Tomorrow..." Matt chuckled. "Scratch that. Later this morning, some of us are going on a run for food and supplies. When we're scavenging, we'll keep an eye out for Randy and the other Emperors."

"I want to go."

Well, crap. Of course he did. But he was only fourteen.

When Matt didn't answer, Dylan added, "I need to learn how."

Matt thought about going to the Home Depot with Derrick back in Utah. It seemed ages ago, although it had only been a couple of weeks. They'd run in to those three men, one of whom had been ready to shoot Matt because he'd thought Matt had been watching him. The man had believed that since society had collapsed, he could do anything to anyone. The thought of taking Dylan away from the relative safety of the farm made Matt distinctly nervous, but he knew Dylan was right. He needed to learn. Still, Matt didn't want to commit. "No promises. I don't know yet what will be happening."

"So, that's a maybe?"

The unadulterated hope in Dylan's voice was impossible to miss. Praying Jessica wouldn't kill him for promising even that much, Matt reached over and ruffled Dylan's hair. "That's a maybe."

Dylan pumped a fist in the air. "Yes."

Matt just hoped they could get through the next day with no one getting hurt and without running into any bad guys—specifically, the Emperors.

CHAPTER SIX

Derrick

KEEPING his eyes peeled and his head on a swivel, Derrick drove up the long, dirt road that led to a neighboring farmhouse. That morning after breakfast—fresh eggs from the chickens—Frank had mapped out where nearby houses were and marked the ones where he was pretty sure no one was around. After that, everyone had gotten together and decided to send Derrick, Matt, and Dylan out to look for food and supplies while the others protected the farm.

Now, as the house they were about to check came into view, Derrick scanned the area for any movement, hopeful they would be successful in finding food. "No one around."

"No red X on the door," Matt said from the passenger seat. "Someone could be home."

With a nod of acknowledgement, Derrick said, "We'll be careful." He parked his truck and led the way up the porch steps, knocking loudly on the front door. When no one answered, he knocked once again. Still no response. He peered into the nearest window. Nothing but furniture. Looking toward Matt and Dylan, who had their hands cupped to the glass of another window, he asked, "Anything?"

Matt turned to him. "I don't think anyone's home."

He agreed, but even so, he approached the front door with caution. There could very well be someone hiding on the other side with a rifle locked and loaded, ready to blow the head off of whomever dared to enter.

Matt and Dylan pressed their backs to the wall on the opposite side of the front door from Derrick. He reached for the doorknob. It turned easily. Exhaling sharply, Derrick gave the door a shove, then pressed his back to the wall, out of the line of potential fire. There was no blast, no sound of the slide of a gun being pulled back. Just the sweet trill of a bird resting on the branch of one of the many trees in the yard.

"Can we go in?" Dylan whispered, clearly eager to do what they'd come to do.

Derrick held up a hand to indicate that Matt and Dylan should wait, then he poked his head around the door frame. Not a whisper of movement inside. With a single nod to Matt and Dylan, Derrick stepped through the doorway, his gun leading the way as his gaze swept the living room. Sunlight beamed in through the front windows, illuminating the fine layer of dust that covered all of the wood surfaces— coffee and side tables, entertainment center, dining room table. No streaks from a finger running across the surface could be seen. It appeared no one had been inside for a while.

Optimistic that they might actually find something useful, Derrick instructed Matt and Dylan to search the bedrooms and bathrooms while he searched the kitchen.

Despite hoping for a well-stocked pantry, when Derrick opened the door and saw a single can of green beans, he released a sigh. But it was followed immediately by a cock of his head. Someone had emptied the pantry and left the one can on purpose. Why? As a taunt? Or maybe a warning? To let the next person know that someone bigger and stronger had been there?

The Emperors. It had to be. Especially after Walter reported that they'd raided his farm a few nights earlier. They'd been here and they'd cleared it out.

Would Frank and Sarah's farm be next?

Clenching his jaw, Derrick shook his head. As long as he had anything to do with it, Frank and Sarah's farm would not be harmed.

Derrick searched the rest of the kitchen but found nothing useful and no other food.

"Find anything?" Matt asked as he and Dylan walked into the kitchen.

Derrick held up the can of green beans with a wry smile. "Just this."

Narrowing his eyes, Matt stared at the can. "Just that? Nothing else?"

"Nope. And I'll give you one guess who left it."

"The Emperors," Dylan said with a tone of disdain.

Pleased that Dylan had come to the same conclusion, Derrick tossed him the can, which he easily caught. "Yep." Then he noticed Matt holding a bag. "What'd you find?"

Matt opened the bag and reached inside with a chuckle, pulling out a handful of sample sizes of toothpaste and dental floss. "Jessica will be happy."

That's right. She was a dental hygienist. "Guess the Emperors don't care about dental hygiene."

Matt dropped the items back in the bag with a grin. "Here's to hoping they all get cavities. Big ones that rot their teeth right out of their head."

His shoulders shaking with laughter, Derrick shook his head. "Come on. Let's check the barn."

The smell hit them when they were still a good distance away. Derrick was about to tell Dylan to wait outside, but if the kid wanted to go on these runs, he'd have to get used to the reality in which they now lived. They would see dead bodies. Lots of them. Some dead from the bird flu, others from... well, from any number of reasons. Although as he stopped in front of the man-door that led into the barn—the main door was basically a garage door that he couldn't open from the outside—he suspected the bodies he was about to find had been murdered by whomever had taken all the food.

He tugged the bandana from around his neck to cover his nose and mouth, not that it would do much good. He looked at Matt and Dylan, who had covered their mouths as well. Dylan's eyes were huge as he and Matt nodded.

Bracing himself, Derrick pulled the door open and stepped over the threshold. It was pitch black inside—the only light coming from the open door behind him. Flicking on the flashlight he'd brought along, Derrick breathed shallowly.

"It really stinks," Dylan added. "Is it because there's a...a body in here?"

Sweeping the beam of the flashlight across the spacious interior, Derrick saw several pieces of farming equipment. Taking a tentative step forward, it didn't take long for him to find the source of the stench. A man and woman were crumpled on the concrete floor, puddles of dried blood surrounding them. He brushed the beam across their bodies and saw several bullet holes. They'd been murdered, just as he'd expected.

"The Emperors?" Matt asked.

"Seems likely, although it could've been anyone. But I'm not taking them off the suspect list."

"Me either."

Wanting to do the decent thing, Derrick searched for and found shovels and the three of them buried the couple in the backyard.

CHAPTER SEVEN

Matt

"WE SHOULD HEAD INTO TOWN," Derrick said.

Matt nodded. They'd been to a handful of nearby farms and each one had had the same result. No food. But at least they hadn't come across any other bodies.

They stood beside Derrick's truck in the shade of a tree, drinking water from the bottles they'd brought along. They were parked in the driveway of a house they'd just searched.

"My guess," Matt said as he screwed the lid back on his water bottle, "is that they're hitting unoccupied houses. I think they came across that couple in the first house by mistake. Probably thought the place was abandoned until they went into the barn."

Derrick nodded. "Makes sense. Although the Emperors hit Walter's place. And it was occupied."

Matt nodded. Then a new thought occurred to him. "Maybe they thought Walter's place was empty and when they found it occupied they changed plans. Took his grandkids. Maybe that wasn't the original plan."

"Could be."

Matt desperately hoped his theory was correct. If it was, then all they had to do was make it clear that their farm had many people there. They had to make the farm an unattractive target. But first they needed to find food. There was no way they could come back empty-handed. Not on their first run. They had to prove to Frank and Sarah that they would be an asset. Besides, they'd brought a lot of mouths to feed. They had to provide for themselves.

"Can we stop at houses along the way to town?" Dylan asked.

"Sure," Matt said, then he looked at Derrick to see if he agreed.

Derrick shrugged. "Why not? Maybe we'll get lucky."

Matt hoped so. Thus far the trip had been a bust—except for the toothpaste and dental floss. He smiled at the thought.

Derrick slapped the hood of his truck. "Let's roll."

Dylan jumped into the bench seat in back before Matt climbed in the passenger seat.

"Frank said if we went into populated areas, to head south," Matt said when they reached the end of the gravel drive. "To the north is Stockton. According to Frank, it wasn't the safest place before society collapsed. So now..." He let his words trail off.

"Right." Derrick turned south.

Dylan leaned forward. "Maybe that's where the Emperors are. In Stockton."

If Stockton had been filled with gang-bangers before the apocalypse, then yeah, it made sense that the ones who'd survived had banded together to create this new ultra-gang. "Maybe."

"We should go there," Dylan said, his voice filled with intensity. "To find them."

Matt glanced at Derrick, who was slowly shaking his head, his wrist resting lightly on the steering wheel.

"Come on, Dad."

As angry as Matt was for what the Emperors had done— to him and to Walter—he had zero desire to hunt down Randy and his crew. "Today we're after food and supplies."

Dylan slumped back into his seat.

"Your dad's right," Derrick said, his eyes going to Dylan in the rearview mirror. "We don't need to seek out trouble. It'll find us soon enough." His eyes went back to the road.

Remembering that the Emperors had forced them off of the freeway before robbing them, they decided to stay to the back roads. They were about fifteen miles south of where they'd had their run-in with the Emperors, but still, no reason to chance running in to them again.

"There's a house," Matt said, pointing to a structure tucked away behind tall trees. No other houses were nearby, and the lot looked like it was a couple of acres. "Let's check it out."

Derrick slowed. "Okay."

As Derrick pulled into the circular driveway, Matt scanned the area. No people and no cars. Still, for all they knew a whole family was inside. They would have to approach carefully.

Matt stepped out of the truck, his eyes on the front door. No movement. No red X either. "Anyone home?" he shouted. Leading the way to the front door, he wondered if this would be a waste of time. Maybe they should have driven right past and hit a grocery store instead. Except the nearest grocery store was several miles away while this house was right here.

He knocked loudly, then paused to listen for approaching footsteps. There were none. He twisted the doorknob, but it was locked. With a look at Derrick and a nod of agreement, Matt led the way down the porch steps and toward the back. No fence blocked off the backyard. As they strode toward the back door, Matt was on high alert. Worried that the home-owner was tending a garden or something, he called out, "Hello? Anyone home?"

When there was no answering reply, Dylan said, "Guess not."

Matt climbed the three steps to the deck. Then, trying to see inside, he squinted as he got near the back door, staring at the French doors. No movement came from inside. Just to be safe, he knocked, then pounded on the glass. All was quiet.

He turned the knob. Locked.

Suppressing a sigh, he turned to Dylan. "Find a large rock."

Dylan's eyes widened. Up to this point they'd been able to get into the houses they'd searched through an unlocked door or an open window. Of course, all of those houses had been hit by someone else first. Guess whoever had cleaned out the places hadn't felt the need to lock up afterwards.

Did that mean this house hadn't been hit yet?

Hope blossomed inside Matt.

"We're going to break the glass?" Dylan asked, his eyebrows high on his forehead.

"Unless you have a better idea how we can get in."

Dylan glanced around, his gaze going to the closed windows before settling on the French doors. Shrugging, he turned and walked away.

Matt met Derrick's smiling face with a chuckle.

Moments later Dylan was back with a sizable rock. He held it out to the two men.

Derrick looked at Dylan with a smirk. "You try first."

Dylan's gaze went to Matt, who nodded, then he drew his hand back and lobbed the rock at the glass. It bounced right off. He tried several more times with no luck.

Panting lightly, he turned to Matt and Derrick. "How about I try to break a window instead?"

Matt nodded with approval. "Good idea. A window should be a lot easier to break."

Dylan chose a large window that would be fairly easy to climb through and hurled the rock right at the glass. It shattered immediately, leaving jagged edges that looked wicked enough to slice them all to ribbons.

Using a cushion from a nearby chair, Matt cleared all of the glass out of the frame, then turned to Dylan and Derrick with a grin. "I'll climb in."

CHAPTER EIGHT

Matt

THE PLACE WAS SURPRISINGLY CLEAN. Not even much dust. How long had the residents been gone? Then a new thought popped into Matt's head. Maybe whoever lived there was out scavenging too. Maybe they would be back any minute.

With a new sense of urgency, Matt hustled to the French doors and let Derrick and Dylan inside.

"I'll check the bedrooms and bathrooms," Derrick offered.

With a nod, Matt and Dylan headed to the kitchen. The first thing Matt noticed was how tidy the room was. The only things on the counters were a toaster, a can opener, and a bowl of oranges. Matt went directly to the oranges, picking one up. Mold had formed where the orange in his hand had been touching the ones beneath it.

"That answers that question," he murmured.

"What question?" Dylan asked as he joined him at the counter.

Matt set the orange back in the bowl and looked at his son. "When we got here, I wondered if the people who live here were out scavenging and would be returning. But the rotting oranges tell me that they've been gone a long time."

Dylan nodded. "Because if the people were still around, they would have eaten the oranges or thrown them out."

"Yep." Hope growing that no one would be showing up anytime soon, Matt strode to the pantry. He pulled the door open then turned to Dylan in triumph. "Score!"

Smiling, Dylan came to stand beside him and looked at the shelves heavy with food. Boxes of crackers, cookies, macaroni and cheese mix, spaghetti noodles. Jars of spaghetti sauce, cans of soup and vegetables. Bags of flour and sugar.

Barely able to withhold his joy, Matt said, "Sarah will be able to make her bread."

"Yes!"

Matt laughed, then he glanced around. "We need a box or something to carry this food in."

"Maybe there are boxes in the garage."

"Good idea."

Grinning, Dylan said, "I'll check."

Matt nodded, and as Dylan left the room, Matt opened other cupboards to see what else he could find. Moments later Dylan shouted, "Dad!"

Heart racing at the tone of Dylan's voice, Matt tore out of the kitchen and ran down the hallway to the garage door where Dylan had his back pressed against the closed door that led to the garage. Derrick got there a moment later.

"What is it?" Matt asked.

Eyes wide, Dylan said, "Someone's in the garage. Sitting in the car."

Alarmed, Matt shoved Dylan away from the door. Whoever was out there was probably armed and could shoot right through the door. But it didn't make sense. The oranges were rotten. Was it a trick? A ploy to make people think no one was home? Was the person in the garage trying to lure people in? But why?

"Get back," Derrick said, then he drew his gun out of his waist holster and moved to the side. "Okay. Open the door."

Despite being worried that they were stepping into a trap, Matt did as Derrick asked, yanking the door open. When nothing happened, Derrick swung his gun into the opening, then poked his head around the door frame before pulling back. Still nothing.

"Are you sure someone was there?" Derrick said to Dylan, his voice low.

Looking less certain, Dylan shrugged and nodded at the same time.

Matt didn't hear any noise coming from the garage. "It might be a trap."

Derrick nodded, but stepped into the garage nonetheless. Matt drew his weapon, told Dylan to wait there, then followed Derrick, who had turned on his flashlight.

Matt immediately saw that Dylan was right. A man was sitting behind the wheel of a car.

Aiming his gun at the man, Derrick approached the driver side door. "Hands where I can see them!"

The man didn't move. Not a muscle. That's when a familiar odor hit Matt. "I think he's dead."

Derrick nodded. "Yeah. I do too." He holstered his weapon and opened the car door.

The stench hit Matt full-on. He threw his hand over his nose and mouth.

Derrick shut the door and manually opened the large garage door, sliding it on its rails. Sunlight and fresh air poured in.

Eyes watering from the smell, Matt hustled to the driveway to be able to breathe the clean air. That's when he saw a hose going from the exhaust pipe to the interior of the car. He shook his head. "Killed himself."

Dylan joined them just outside the garage. "What do you mean?"

Matt pointed to the hose. "He poisoned himself with the exhaust fumes."

Dylan looked confused. "But the car's not on."

Derrick pulled the hose out of the exhaust pipe. "Must've run out of gas." He looked at Matt and Dylan. "Died a while ago, I guess."

Matt knew things were bad, but were they so awful that it was worth taking your own life? Then again, he didn't know what this man had lost. Maybe his whole family. If

Matt's whole family was dead, what would he do? He honestly didn't know, so he wasn't about to judge. "We should bury him."

Derrick frowned. "I don't really want to take the time."

Neither did Matt, but he had a good reason. "We're going to take all of his food. It's the least we can do."

Sighing, Derrick nodded. "All right."

They found shovels and took turns digging a shallow grave for the man before wrapping him in a sheet and laying him in the hole. They covered him with dirt, then set rocks on top to discourage animals from digging him up. After a moment of silence, they went back in the garage and got to work, finding several boxes that they dumped out. Before long they'd emptied the entire pantry and loaded all of the food into the bed of Derrick's truck. They also took toiletries and medications they found, along with a few other supplies that had caught their eye.

"Nice haul," Derrick said as they drove away from the house.

Matt shoved aside the image of the dead man while at the same time saying a silent prayer of thanks that he'd left such a bounty for them to enjoy.

A short distance down the road they came to another house. Derrick looked at Matt with raised eyebrows. Matt nodded. Derrick pulled into the drive. The front door had a bright red X painted on it.

"What do you think?" Matt asked. "Should we see what we can find?"

Dylan leaned forward, hovering over the console between the two front seats. "But there will be dead bodies inside."

Derrick looked at Dylan. "Which means there might be food." He smirked. "Dead people don't eat."

Matt nodded. "It's worth a look." He pointed to the bandana on the seat next to Dylan. "Mask up."

The three of them put their bandanas over their mouths and noses, then jumped out of the truck.

CHAPTER NINE

Derrick

DERRICK WAS eager to get the food and get out. Though he'd gotten used to the stink of death, he wanted to minimize his exposure to bodies that possibly carried the deadly virus. He didn't know how long the virus could live on a corpse and he had no desire to find out.

Before approaching the front door, he swept his gaze across the front of the house. Blinds were down on all the windows. No way to tell if anyone was inside. Anyone living, that is.

Resting his hand on the butt of his gun in his waist holster, he mounted the porch steps then ran his finger across the red paint. The X was bone dry. No telling how long it had been there. He knocked, loud and sure, then waited. No response.

Doubting the door was unlocked, he turned the knob anyway. To his surprise, the door opened. The stench of death slapped him in the face, making him recoil. The bandana did little to dampen the smell, but that wasn't really its purpose. It was for protection from germs that might somehow get into his nasal passages.

Before stepping inside, Derrick turned to Matt and Dylan, whose eyes were scrunched up in clear disgust. "I don't think we have to worry about anyone living."

Matt shook his head. "Nope."

Derrick let his gaze slide to Dylan, who looked like he might hurl. Figuring the body or bodies would be in the bedroom, Derrick offered to search that part of the house. Eventually though, the kid would have to face the nastiness of a corpse decomposing from the virus. "Let's get this over with."

With a curt nod, they split up. Derrick made his way up the stairs. The foul odor grew stronger. Ignoring it, he did a quick search of the first bedroom—no bodies there. He didn't find anything worth taking. Same story in the next bedroom and in the hall bathroom. Finally, he walked toward the master bedroom. The strength of the smell told him that that was where the body was. Sure enough, sprawled in the middle of the bed was a bloated, rotting corpse.

Averting his gaze, he searched the master bathroom before turning to the room itself. Gagging a bit and in a hurry to leave, he forced his eyes to stay on the bedside tables. The first one held nothing of interest, but the second one held a handgun. Brightening with his find, he tucked the gun in the back of his jeans then did a quick search of the dresser. Several boxes of ammo were nestled in the bottom drawer.

Thrilled, he gathered every box into his arms and hustled down the stairs to see what Matt and Dylan had found.

They'd already filled a box with food from the pantry. It wasn't nearly as much as they'd found in the last house, but every bit would help. Derrick dumped the ammo on the counter and smiled, although he knew they couldn't see his expression behind the bandana.

Matt nodded. "Nice!"

Soon, they were back on the road, their bandanas off. Flush with success, when another house appeared, Derrick didn't even ask. He just pulled into the driveway, then hopped out of the car. Matt and Dylan were right behind him. He lifted his fist to knock, but before his knuckle touched the wood, the door flew open. The only thing he saw was the shotgun pointed at his face.

"Get off my property," the man holding the gun growled.

Momentarily stunned, Derrick met the man's gaze, then he threw his hands up. "Okay, okay. We're leaving.

The man motioned with his shotgun for them to get going.

Not wanting to turn his back on the man, Derrick slowly retreated while keeping his eyes on the man and his hands in the air. When he reached the bottom of the porch steps, he turned around. Dylan had already climbed into the back seat and Matt was closing the door on the passenger side. Derrick hurried around the hood of his truck and hopped behind the wheel. Then he looked at the man, whose gun never wavered. Derrick started up the engine and they tore out of there.

"Okay," Derrick said as his racing heart slowed to its normal rate. "Guess we got a little cocky. We have to remember that some houses are occupied."

"Can't really blame the guy," Matt said. "We'd do the same if people showed up at the farm."

That was true. "Speaking of that, we should probably get back. We have a lot to do to secure the farm." Derrick felt like it was up to him to make sure it was done right. True, Jeff had said it wasn't all on him, but he felt like it was, nonetheless.

"Sounds good," Matt said. "We got a decent amount of food." He chuckled. "It won't last long though. Not with how big our group is."

That was painfully true. They would have to either go scavenging several times a week, or they would need to get a bigger haul, something that would carry them for a longer time. At least Frank and Sarah had a decent-sized garden. Which reminded him... "We need to find seeds so we can expand the garden."

Matt made a sound of disgust in his throat.

Derrick squinted at him in confusion. Until he remembered that Matt and Jessica had had a number of seeds. Before the Emperors had taken everything. Lips tugging downward, Derrick wondered how long it would be until they crossed paths with the Emperors. Preferably not for a while. They had enough to do—scavenging, creating a secure perimeter, expanding the garden, building more housing. Not to mention the day-to-day tasks of running a farm and feeding their small army.

Suppressing a sigh, Derrick focused on driving. It didn't take long to reach the turnoff to the farm. They drove down the gravel road toward the house, which was hidden from view by the almond trees in the neighboring orchard, but when they cleared the orchard, Derrick saw two unfamiliar vehicles in the driveway, one truck and one SUV. Immediately on alert, he stopped, put the truck in reverse, then backed all the way down the driveway before driving a short distance away and parking his truck behind some overgrown bushes.

CHAPTER TEN

Matt

DEEPLY CONCERNED ABOUT who was at the farm, especially since his family was there, Matt's thoughts flew in a hundred directions at once. He stared at Derrick. "Who do you think it is?"

Derrick shook his head.

Maybe it was Walter again, although there were two vehicles. What if it was the Emperors? No one had been outside. Wait. Wasn't someone supposed to be on watch? For all Matt knew, his family was in serious danger. He reached for his door. "We need to go." He hopped out.

"Hang on," Derrick said.

This annoyed Matt. Derrick didn't have any family inside. Then again, weren't they all family now? Deciding to listen to Derrick, Matt paused, standing just outside the passenger door. "What?"

"We need to approach with caution. From a direction no one would expect. Scope out who's there and see what's happening."

Okay. That made sense. Still, Matt ground his teeth together. If his family was in danger, every second counted.

Derrick got out of the truck, a pair of binoculars in hand. Then Dylan stepped onto the ground. Matt scrutinized his son. He didn't want to put him in harm's way. Should he have him wait in the truck? Or would that expose him to some unknown risk that Matt hadn't even considered? Better to have him come along where Matt could keep an eye on him. They would stay to the trees in the neighboring orchard. With any luck, whoever was at Frank and Sarah's house would never know they were under surveillance.

Matt gestured to the fence. "There's barbed wire. Do you have anything we can throw over it?"

Nodding, Derrick dug around in the bed of the truck, pulling out a couple of towels they'd taken from one of the houses they'd scavenged. Derrick folded them lengthwise, then laid them across the barbed wire before carefully climbing over. Matt and Dylan followed, managing to get over the fence without injury. Matt picked up the towels, curling them around his shoulders for later use—the entire property was surrounded by barbed wire fencing.

Letting Derrick take point, Matt motioned for Dylan to follow before taking up the rear. They made their way deep into the orchard so as to be less visible from Frank and Sarah's property. The almond trees were well on their way to full blossoms, giving them fairly decent cover.

Keeping his ears tuned for any sound that didn't belong, Matt continually glanced toward the house while making sure he didn't walk into a tree or trip over anything on the ground.

They'd gone less than a hundred yards when Derrick held his fist up as he stopped in place, then he crouched. Matt was about to press a hand on Dylan's shoulder to make sure he crouched too, but when Dylan did it without urging, Matt smiled and hunkered down. Only then did Matt turn his focus to what had caught Derrick's attention.

Not fifty feet away, a man with a semi-automatic rifle slung over his shoulder was walking the perimeter of the farm's property as if he were on watch. A man they'd never seen before.

Alarmed, Matt looked at Derrick. Derrick shifted his eyes to Matt, his expression conveying the same questions sliding through Matt's mind—Who was this guy? Where were *their* people? What was going on?

They stayed in place until the man had passed. Once he was a good distance away and his back was to them, Derrick nodded. The three of them stood and crept forward.

The man on patrol disappeared around the side of the house. The trio took advantage of his absence, dashing through the orchard to a better vantage point.

"This'll work," Derrick muttered as he knelt on the dirt and lifted the binoculars to his eyes, the lenses pointed to the windows across the back of the house. He stared for several moments, then silently handed the binocs to Matt, who had knelt as well.

Matt pressed them to his eyes, staring at the scene inside the house, searching for his family. Not everyone from their group was visible, but there was Jessica. She was sitting on the couch beside Emily and Sarah, her expression showing a mix of concern and concentration, like she was listening very closely to whatever the speaker was saying. Matt's eyes tracked to the person Jessica was listening to, but his back was to the window.

The others within view looked calm. That was reassuring. He handed the binocs to Dylan, then turned to Derrick. "What do you think? Should we go inside?"

"No. We don't know who these guys are or what they want. I don't want to reveal our existence. Jeff and Chris know that when we see those trucks we'll back off and recon rather than come inside. If asked, they won't admit we exist." He grinned. "Let's not turn them into liars."

Though Matt would have preferred to be by his wife's side, what Derrick said made sense. He nodded.

Derrick took the binocs from Dylan. "Unless things go south, we stay here until they leave."

CHAPTER ELEVEN

Jessica

JESSICA WISHED MATT WAS THERE. Not only was she worried about his safety while he was away, but with these men showing up for who knew what purpose, she was very nervous. They claimed they were from the state government, but something about their demeanor reminded her of the neighborhood cooperative they'd escaped. It didn't help that the moment these guys had arrived they'd taken everyone's guns with the promise that they could have them back once they left.

Jeff had nearly shot one of the men until another man had held a gun to Sarah's head. Only then had Jeff and the others given up their weapons, although the tension had been sky high and remained so.

Jessica was still unclear how the men had gotten onto the property in the first place, although she suspected they'd driven in when whoever was on watch had been on the opposite side of the fairly large property, basically sneaking in. She was certain Jeff and Chris had already realized that having only one person on watch would not be enough. Especially when the gate was open as it had been since Matt, Dylan, and Derrick were out scavenging.

Four men had come. One was standing in front of them. Taller than average and with an athletic build, he wore a ball cap on his head along with jeans and a t-shirt. He also wore a gun in a shoulder holster. Another man—armed, of course— stood nearby. That man faced them like he wanted to keep an eye on them, like he would stop them if they tried to leave. Like he wouldn't mind shooting someone. A third man was walking the property—Jessica had seen him stroll past twice now. A fourth man had come inside initially, but in the shuffle of gathering everyone, he'd vanished. Jessica figured he was searching the house while the other two kept them occupied. But as far as she knew, Frank and Sarah didn't have any kind of stash for the men to steal. Still, it was disturbing to have strangers freely roaming the house and property like they had full rights to be there.

The men had only been there long enough to gather Jessica and the rest of her group in one place. For what purpose, she had no idea.

She glanced at Jeff. His arms were crossed over his chest, his lips were flat, and his eyes were snapping with fury.

"Now that everyone's here," the man who stood in front of them said, "let's get started. My name's Owen." He broke out into a smile. "No need to look so nervous. We're simply here on government business."

"What kind of government business?" Jeff's voice boomed out.

Owen's gaze went to Jeff, his smile growing. "With so many people dying from the bird flu, we need to take a census to see who is still among us."

Jeff's eyes narrowed. "Why?"

Owen's smile faltered. Maybe he wasn't used to people questioning his request. After all, what harm was there in taking a census? Unless it gave the government information that could be used against its citizens.

"To provide services, of course," Owen said smoothly, like he'd rehearsed that line.

"What kinds of services?" Chris asked. His tone was markedly friendlier than Jeff's. Were he and Jeff playing good cop bad cop?

Owen shifted his eyes to Chris, his shoulders relaxing like he didn't feel any hostility from Chris like he had from Jeff. "Many people are starving. If food is needed, the government wants to know."

Jessica's heart skipped a beat. This was reminiscent of the neighborhood cooperative. "Are you going to provide food? And if you do, what do you want in return?"

All eyes swiveled to her.

"We're getting ahead of ourselves," Owen said, which alarmed Jessica. His non-answer made her wonder if he was sincere about his purposes. Was he really even from the government? Then again, did it matter? Society had collapsed. As far as she was concerned, they were on their own. Yet, if he really was from the government, maybe he could provide help. They were low on food.

"Now," Owen said as his gaze swept over the group, "I see thirteen people. Is that everyone who lives here?"

Jessica's thoughts shot to Matt, Dylan, and Derrick. Should they admit the three of them lived there too but were gone at the moment?

"That's everyone," Jeff said before anyone else could speak.

Okay. Jeff thought they shouldn't tell them the truth. That was fine with her. The less these people knew about them the better. Jessica looked at Kayla and Brooke, who both looked uncertain about the lie. She stared at them until they met her gaze. After a moment of meeting her eyes, they both looked at the floor, apparently getting the message to not say anything about their father and brother and Derrick.

Owen scrutinized each person to see if anyone would disagree with Jeff. When no one did, he took a small notepad and pencil out of his back pocket and wrote on it. "All right." He looked up at them. "What are your food needs?"

"We're good," Jeff said, again before anyone else could speak.

Owen stared at him like that wasn't what he'd expected to hear. Just then, the missing man appeared. He strode into the room and said something to Owen that Jessica couldn't hear. Owen nodded. The man left the room and a few moments later Jessica saw him approaching the man who'd been patrolling.

Jeff stood, which startled everyone, including the armed man standing in the corner who reached for the gun at his hip. Thankfully, he just rested his hand on the butt of his gun.

"What do you people really want?" Jeff asked.

Owen tilted his head as his eyebrows bunched. "What do you mean? We care about the citizens of California. We've lost way too many people already and don't want to lose any more. Especially if there's something we can do to prevent it."

He seemed sincere, but Jessica had her doubts.

"As you can see," Jeff said, "we're doing fine." He held his arm toward the front door. "Thanks for stopping by."

Owen ignored Jeff and looked at Frank and Sarah. "This is your home. What are your thoughts?"

Jeff was left standing there. He dropped his arm to his side and looked at Frank.

Frank sat up straighter and cleared his throat. "What are you doing about those Emperors?"

Frowning, Owen shook his head. "We've heard about them and know they've caused a bit of trouble in this area."

"They're stealing from people and kidnapping children. What are you going to do about it?"

Owen's forehead creased. "Kidnapping children? That sounds a bit far-fetched."

Frank got to his feet, his expression fierce. "It's not far-fetched at all. Two of my neighbor's grandkids were kidnapped just the other night."

CHRISTINE KERSEY

Owen nodded like he was considering the terribleness of the crime. "I'll be sure and report it to my superiors."

Making a scoffing sound, Frank sat back on his recliner. "You're useless."

Owen's mouth fell open as if he were offended. "Our job is simply to gather information."

What worried Jessica was the type of information they were gathering and what they would do with it.

When no one else spoke, Owen looked at the guard who'd been standing quietly in the corner and gestured with his head toward the front door, then Owen turned and smiled at the assembled group. "Thank you for your cooperation."

Moments later they were gone.

"Like we had a choice," Jeff growled as he made a beeline for the kitchen where the men had set everyone's weapons, grabbing his gun and holstering it.

CHAPTER TWELVE

Matt

THE SECOND THE truck and SUV were gone, Matt hustled to the fence, laid the towel across the barbed wire on top, and climbed over. Hardly waiting for Dylan and Derrick, he raced to the back porch, yanking the door open the moment he reached it.

As he stepped inside, his eyes went right to Jessica. To his great relief, she was fine, as were Brooke and Kayla.

Jessica leapt to her feet and rushed toward him. "Matt!"

As he embraced her, Dylan came through the door.

Pulling away, Matt asked Jessica, "What'd they want?"

Her eyebrows shot up. "You saw them?"

He laughed. "Yeah. Why do you think I came in right after they left?"

She smiled, her eyes tight. "Right, right."

He turned to Dylan. "Where's Derrick?"

"Getting the truck."

Good. They'd collected a lot of valuable items—including food. Best to get it unloaded and put away as soon as possible.

Jessica stood in front of him, her forehead furrowed. "They said they were from the state government."

That explained why things had been calm. If it had been the Emperors, he was sure it would have been a much different story. He glanced toward the family room where everyone was gathered. Some people were still sitting and some were standing, but nearly everyone was talking.

Jeff walked over to Matt and Jessica, his eyebrows tugging together. "Where's Derrick?"

Matt explained.

Nodding, Jeff said, "We need to talk." He led the way to the front door, opened it, and stepped onto the wide porch. Matt and Jessica followed. Moments later, Chris and Emily joined them.

"Let's wait for Derrick," Jeff said as he looked toward the gravel road. He turned to Matt. "Did you have much luck?"

Forcing away thoughts of the people they'd buried, Matt nodded with a grim smile. "Yep. Found some food and other things."

Derrick's truck rumbled up the road, stopping in front of the garage. The five of them went to meet him.

Derrick got out and faced them. "Glad to see everyone's still healthy." He stared at Jeff. "And that no one got shot."

Jeff frowned. "I nearly shot the idiot who just left but one of his men threatened to shoot Sarah. That's when they took our guns. Temporarily."

That sent a zing of alarm charging through Matt. Those men had meant business. And they weren't stupid. "Jessica said they were from the government. What did they want?"

Jeff crossed his arms. "Claimed to be taking a census. Said they wanted to make sure everyone had enough food."

Matt nodded at the truck. "There's food out there to be found."

Jeff chuckled. "That's what I figured, which is why I told them we were good." He grinned. "I also told them that everyone in that room was all the people we had."

Matt glanced at Derrick, who smiled like he was saying *What did I tell you?*

"But that one guy searched the house," Jessica said. "Maybe they're going to come back when we least expect it and take whatever they want." She chewed on her lip. "Sound familiar?"

Matt flashed back to the neighborhood cooperative back home, understanding Jessica's concern. If those men were anything like those bullies had been, they would have a fight ahead of them. And they didn't even know where the men had come from. "How'd they get on the property? I mean, did we let them in?" This was something he'd been thinking about ever since they'd gotten back from their scavenging run and had found the vehicles at the house.

"I was wondering the same thing," Derrick said.

Jeff frowned deeply. "The gate was open, which was a

mistake. We need to keep it closed and locked at all times. Even if someone's out on a run. And the property's spread out. We need to have more than one person on watch to make sure the front and back are always covered." He scowled. "They came in through the front gate when I was around back."

"Look," Derrick said, "we made a mistake, but we won't make the same one twice."

Jeff chuckled. "No. We'll make all new ones."

That brought a round of laughter, which eased the tense mood.

"What should we do about them?" Emily asked, bringing their thoughts back to the men who'd arrived uninvited.

"Not a whole lot we can do," Jeff said. "We don't know where they're based. We don't even know it they're legit from the government." He shook his head and sighed audibly. "All we can do is see if they make contact again." He grimaced. "And be ready for them if they do."

"Oh, they will," Chris said as his gaze swept the property. "At least two of their men searched the place. No doubt they found things they'd like to take." He looked back at the group. "They'd probably like to take our weapons too. Then we would become easy pickings."

Matt hoped Chris was wrong. Maybe they really were just taking a census so they could help. But he feared his optimism was misplaced. "What if we block the road? You know, get a box truck or something."

"Great idea," Derrick said. "I remember seeing one today."

He chuckled. "I think I even remember where it was." He paused. "But first, let's get this food unloaded."

With help from nearly everyone, it didn't take long to bring their spoils inside.

"How far did you travel to find this?" Sarah asked Matt as he helped her sort the items into categories.

"Not far. Maybe five miles."

Her face brightened. "I'm glad some folks stocked their pantries." Then her positive expression began to fade.

Matt knew what she was thinking. For their group to benefit, someone else had to suffer. He thought of the unpleasant things he'd seen on the run. Mentally shaking the images away, he smiled at Sarah. "I'm sure those that bought it would be glad to know it's helping others survive."

Still somber, Sarah nodded as she continued putting the food away.

When they were done, Matt went with Derrick to the place where Derrick remembered seeing a box truck. It was parked haphazardly on the side of the road, and as a bonus, the keys had been left on the console between the seats. The back of the truck was empty though.

Matt drove the box truck back to the farm while Derrick drove his truck. Once back, Matt positioned the box truck behind the closed and locked gate in such a way that no one would be able to drive up the road to the farm's property. People could approach on foot—nothing they could do to prevent that. But blocking the road would certainly slow down any uninvited visitors.

CHAPTER THIRTEEN

Matt

OVER THE NEXT week they began to fall into a routine—
working in the garden and fruit orchard, collecting eggs from
the chicken coop, milking the few cows that produced milk,
caring for the horses, patrolling the property, preparing meals
and cleaning up. They also spent hours each day on weapons
training. Under the tutelage of Derrick, Jeff, and Chris,
everyone but the three little children took lots of target prac-
tice and trained on what they would do if they came under
attack. Matt could see that Jessica and his children were
becoming much more comfortable with their guns, which
pleased him.

As each person took on chores, they each began to figure
out what they liked to do. Matt was no exception. He definitely enjoyed patrolling, but that was only for a few hours
each day. The rest of the time he worked with others to

prepare the ground for expanding the garden, chopped fire-wood, went on several runs to gather more food and supplies, and any number of other tasks that came up.

By the end of each day, he was exhausted. More tired than he ever had been working as a software engineer. And when everyone gathered in the evening, hot and tired from working all day, it became obvious that there were too many people living in too small a space. People would get grumpy and the feeling would spread like a virus until the tension in the house was palpable.

No one wanted to complain—Matt in particular was extremely grateful for Frank and Sarah's generosity in giving them a chance to prove themselves—but it had to be said. One night after the dinner dishes had been cleaned up, Matt asked if everyone would meet outside under the covered patio for a meeting.

When he asked, Jessica cocked an eyebrow at him in ques-tion, but he just smiled, took her hand, and led the way outside. Once everyone except Chris and Emily, who were patrolling, were seated, Matt stood and faced the group. As he looked at the faces of the people he considered his family, warmth spread through his chest. These were good people, people who had his back and he had theirs. These were chal-lenging times, but they would make it. Together.

"What's this all about?" Frank asked.

Matt shifted his gaze to the man he'd learned to respect more and more over the week they'd been there. Frank had so much knowledge about how to run things—knowledge that

Matt was sorely lacking. Frank was a good man, a generous man.

"First off," Matt said as he smiled at Frank, "I want you to know how much we all appreciate you letting us stay here over the last week."

Heads nodded all around, although Matt noticed Derrick lifting an eyebrow like he was wondering where Matt was going with this.

"I have to admit," Frank said, his voice gruff, "the way everyone has pitched in kind of surprised me." He chuckled. "I'm sorry to say that I had my doubts, but you all," his gaze swept the group, "are hard workers." He scanned the space where they'd expanded the garden and where a huge pile of chopped wood was stacked, then he turned back to Matt. "Sarah and I never could have gotten this much done on our own." He smiled at his wife as he took her hand. "Not even close."

Sarah smiled brightly. "And we have more food now than when you all showed up."

Elated that Frank and Sarah saw the value of their group, Matt gathered his thoughts as he prepared to tell them what he had in mind. He'd mulled over the problem during the last few days and the solution seemed obvious.

"Maybe everyone has noticed," Matt began, "but when we're all in the house, it feels pretty crowded."

He caught Frank and Sarah exchanging a look—one that said they were glad someone was bringing this up because they'd discussed it in private and were all too aware of the issue.

Then Matt looked at the faces of the others and saw that they all felt the same way. He grinned. "Okay. We're all on the same page."

"We're not going to leave, are we Dad?" Kayla asked, her eyes shifting between him and Frank.

Matt looked at Frank to see his response. Though Matt had an idea of how they could solve the crowding problem, he didn't want to step on Frank's toes.

Frank visibly took a breath before slowly exhaling, then he glanced at Sarah, who nodded. Frank smiled. "We want you to stay."

The words were simple but brought a tremendous relief. Matt knew he wasn't the only one silently rejoicing. "Thank you." His words of gratitude were echoed by everyone but the small children. After the group had quieted, Matt smiled. "Now, back to the problem at hand." He paused a beat. "I have an idea for a way to immediately resolve the issue."

All eyes were on him, filled with expectation.

"What if we brought a few RVs here? We could haul a few back here to give each family a separate space for sleeping and, you know, getting away from the group. We'd have instant housing."

Matt could see the wheels turning in everyone's minds. He went on.

"There wouldn't be any water or sewer or power in the RVs, so we'd still need to gather together for meals."

Frank was nodding. "That could work."

Amy, Chris's wife, cleared her throat. "How many RVs are you thinking? I mean, who would get one?"

Matt turned to her, then looked at her two small boys who were playing with toy cars in the dirt nearby. Serena, Paisley's two-year-old daughter, was playing with Amy's boys.

He looked at Amy and then Paisley. "As far as I'm concerned, whoever wants one can have one." He shifted his eyes to Frank. "Assuming there's room to place all of them."

Frank stood and walked a short distance away, stopping just past the edge of the patio, his gaze sweeping the open area near the barn. He stared for several long moments, then turned and faced the group. "I think there's enough room." He grinned. "Never thought I'd be runnin' an RV park." With a soft chuckle, he walked back to his chair and sat down.

Matt held back his own grin. This was going to work. People would have their own space, yet they'd still be together. It was perfect.

CHAPTER FOURTEEN

Jessica

"Sometimes you can be brilliant," Jessica said to Matt as they got ready for bed that night. She smirked. "Although I'm going to miss sleeping on this air mattress."

Matt laughed. "I'll bet you will. Especially when it goes flat in the middle of the night."

Yeah, that was really annoying, although she'd been able to easily overlook it when she considered the other option—being homeless. But having a real bed again would be heavenly.

"I want to go with you tomorrow to get the RVs."

He looked at her with raised eyebrows. "You do?"

She hadn't left the farm since they'd arrived. It was time to get out there, to see what it was like. To help. "If you're picking out our home, then yeah, I want to be part of it."

He laughed. "Ah. I see. You don't trust me to get the right RV."

Shaking her head, she said, "That's not it at all. In case you haven't noticed, I've been kind of holed up here since we got here. I admit it. I've been scared to leave the safety of this place, but I need to push myself and face my fears. How else am I going to get over them?" Besides, she'd been training for days. She was ready.

He stared at her a moment. "All right. If you want to come, that's fine with me." He smiled. "It'll be like before. When we used to run errands together."

That time seemed so long ago. "Except now there will be a lot fewer shoppers. And we won't have to actually pay for anything."

One side of his mouth quirked up in a wry smile. "True."

Jessica didn't sleep well that night, plagued by nightmares of being attacked and shot at. Then she woke up and remembered that those things had actually happened. And she'd survived.

I can do this.

"You awake?" Matt asked from beside her early the next morning.

She shifted to face him. "Yeah."

"You still want to come RV shopping?"

"Yes and no."

Eyebrows tugging together, he said, "You don't have to." His lips pursed. "To be honest, I'd feel better if you were here."

She thought about the men who claimed they were from the government. "It's not necessarily safer here."

Matt grimaced, obviously thinking about the same thing.

"Besides," she said, "I have to do this. For myself and for the girls. Dylan's gone with you, what? Three times? The girls and I need to get out there too. In fact, after I go today I want to go out on a run for food. The girls mentioned that they'd like to go sometime too. It would be good for all of us."

Matt looked less certain, which made Jessica wonder what exactly he'd seen out there. He'd never told her and she hadn't asked. She would find out soon enough.

They joined the others for a breakfast of eggs fresh from the chicken coop and thick slices of bread that Sarah had baked the afternoon before. They were eating well, which made Jessica think about the rest of the people out there. How were they faring? How many people were even left? And how desperate had they become?

"So," Derrick said after breakfast was done, "we'll take my truck, Chris's SUV, and Frank's truck. That will allow us to bring back three trailers."

This was getting real. "Does that mean we'll have to go back out to get the fourth? Or we could get a Class C. We'll have enough drivers. I mean, I could drive one back. Then we'd be done with it."

They'd decided to get four RVs—one for Matt and Jessica's family, one for Chris and Amy's family, one for Paisley and Serena, and one for Derrick. Jeff and Emily would stay in the house with Frank and Sarah.

"Great idea," Derrick said with a nod. "Of course, that assumes we can find the keys."

"They should be stored in the office somewhere," Matt said.

Jessica hoped so. As much as she wanted to do this, she also had deep trepidation. What if someone was guarding the lot? What if they ran in to the Emperors? What if they were attacked on the way there or back? So many things could go wrong.

Don't borrow trouble.

The words her mother used to tell her filled her mind. And her mother was right. Why worry about what might happen? They would deal with it if and when it came up.

"Okay," Matt said. "Let's get this done."

Nodding along with the rest of those going—Matt, Derrick, and Chris—Jessica swallowed her fear and walked with them to the front of the house where the vehicles were parked. Derrick got in his truck, Chris got in his SUV, and Jessica and Matt got in Frank's truck, which was a good twenty years old.

Frank had marked on a map where to go to get to the closest RV dealership. It was only about five miles away. Still, as Jessica and Matt drove through the open gate, which Jeff waited to close behind them, she felt her heart rate pick up a notch.

As they drove, it felt to Jessica that they were going back the way they'd come when they'd first arrived over a week earlier. "Is this the way we came when we got here?"

Matt nodded. "Yep. The closest dealership is this way."

The memory of being accosted by the Emperors washed over her and her heart pounded like a jackhammer in her chest. Where they going right into the Emperors' nest?

CHAPTER FIFTEEN

Derrick

DERRICK HAD AN UNEASY FEELING. Before leaving the farm they'd discussed which RV dealership to go to, and though there were a couple south of the farm—away from the area where they'd had their run-in with the Emperors—those RV dealerships were fifteen miles away. The one they were headed to was only five miles from the farm, although it was north— only a few miles from where the Emperors had held them at gunpoint and taken over half of their stuff. Even so, it had seemed prudent to keep the distance they would travel as short as possible. Less chance for contact with other people. Less chance for conflict.

Derrick had voted for going to this location. An hour ago it had seemed like the best decision. Now though, as they drove through the deserted streets, he had the uneasy sense that they were being watched.

Maybe they should turn around and make the longer trek to a presumably safer area. He picked up the walkie to make the suggestion, but then the RV dealership came into view with several rows of shiny new RVs. Made no sense to turn around and travel twenty miles in the other direction. He pressed the *Talk* button. "There's the dealership. Over."

Matt and Chris both said *Copy*.

Derrick's truck was in the lead. A chain stretched across the driveway to the lot. He stopped in front of it, then got out of his truck. He took a pair of bolt cutters from the back of the truck and removed the obstacle from his path. He tossed the bolt cutters into the bed of his truck and drove onto the lot.

No one was visible, but there were many places someone could hide.

The feeling of being watched had dissipated. Probably his imagination.

Derrick pulled into a parking space and got out of his truck. Matt and Jessica, and then Chris parked as well, joining him.

"How do you want to do this?" Matt asked, his eyes scanning the RVs.

Derrick didn't want to take a long time. "Let's go inside and find where the keys are stored. Then we'll pick out the RVs and get back to the farm."

Matt and Chris nodded. Derrick turned to Jessica. Her gaze was shooting in all directions. Was she hoping to find an

RV like the one they'd had stolen by the Emperors? Or was she nervous?

"See anything you want?"

Her gaze jerked to him. "Uh, not yet."

Okay. It was nerves. That was good. Overconfidence could be dangerous.

"Why don't you and Matt look around? Chris and I will find the keys."

She and Matt nodded and headed off while he and Chris went to the glass doors that fronted the dealership. Hoping they'd get lucky, Derrick tugged on the door. Nope. Locked tight. "Let's check around back for another entrance."

Being cautious, Derrick crept around the side of the building, slowing when a solid door came into view. He stopped in front of it. Someone had shot it open. Saved him the trouble, but was the shooter still there?

Concerned, but not overly so, he motioned to Chris to cover him. Chris was ex-military too. He knew what to do. Confident that Chris had his six, Derrick took a small flashlight out of his back pocket, gripping it in his left hand. With his Glock in his right, he crossed his wrists and moved slowly into the interior of the dark building. He flicked the flashlight on, swept an area, then turned it off. He did this over and over until all the rooms had been cleared.

The place was empty. Whoever had broken the door had come and gone. Maybe they'd had the same idea as Derrick and their group. Didn't matter. They were plenty of RVs left to choose from.

It didn't take long to find where the keys were supposed to be stored. Only problem was, not a single key was in the cabinet. Instead, all he saw were dozens of shiny, empty hooks. Derrick turned to Chris, whose eyes shifted from the empty cabinet to Derrick's face.

Chris shook his head. "Guess whoever owns the place didn't want anyone stealing the RVs."

"Guy's probably dead, so why should he care?"

Chris shrugged.

Certain they could work around this problem, Derrick closed the cabinet. "Let's find Matt and Jessica."

He and Chris headed out to the lot. It took a couple of minutes to find Matt and Jessica, but when he did, he held back a smile. Matt and Jessica stood side by side, admiring a fifth wheel that looked very much like the one they'd had stolen from them.

"Nice," Derrick said.

Jessica spun around like she hadn't heard Derrick and Chris approaching, but when she saw who it was, a grin broke out across her face. Jessica turned back to the fifth wheel. "I'd love to take this one." Her nostrils flared. "But we don't have our truck with its fifth wheel hitch, and none of our trucks have that type of hitch either."

A dark look came over Matt. Derrick knew it still rankled Matt that the Emperors had stolen his truck and RV. After a moment, Matt exhaled sharply, then turned and pointed to an RV that was the size of a city bus. "What about that one?"

Derrick needed to tell them about the new wrinkle. "Before you choose one, I have some bad news."

Jessica's eyebrows tugged together. "What's wrong?"

"There are no keys."

"You mean you couldn't find them?"

He shook his head. "No. I mean someone took all of them."

Jessica turned and slowly scanned all of the RVs within view before facing Matt. "We can still get a bumper-pull, right? I mean, we'll have to jimmy the lock to open the door, but we don't need a key to tow it home, right?"

Matt smiled. "That's right."

Jessica's expression relaxed. "Okay then. Problem solved."

Derrick grinned. He'd figured the problem wasn't insurmountable, and he was gratified to see Jessica pivot so easily. "Perfect."

Jessica led the way to a group of travel trailers, stopping and looking at each one.

"Kind of hard to tell which one would work best for us from the outside," she lamented.

This was taking too long. "You know," Derrick said, not wanting to rush her, but wanting to get this done and leave, "let's just pick three, hook them up, and bring them back to the farm."

Maybe Jessica could sense the tension he was feeling, because her forehead creased. "You're right. Guess I forgot myself for a minute there."

Glad she understood, he smiled. "No problem. So, which ones should we take?"

She pointed to the one she'd been looking over. "This one. Those windows tell me it's a bunkhouse, so there should be plenty of room for the kids." She tapped her chin with her finger, then pointed out another one. "What about that one for you and Amy?" she asked Chris.

"As long as we have a place to sleep, we'll be good."

She pointed to one more. "For Paisley and Serena." Swiveling to Derrick, she said, "What about you?"

He shrugged. "We'll get one for me another time." He didn't really care. His needs were simple, and since they could only take three, it was more important for the families with kids to have a space.

With that resolved, they drove the pair of trucks and the SUV up to the trailers they'd chosen and began hooking them up.

They had just finished when Derrick felt the hairs on his neck stand on end. He straightened, drew his Glock, and spun around.

Not ten feet away stood Emperor Randy and a dozen men, all armed and pointing their weapons at them. Matt, Jessica, and Chris had noticed the Emperors' arrival seconds after Derrick had. Not in time to draw on them though. Only Derrick had his weapon out.

Furious with himself for failing to keep the area secure as they worked, Derrick clenched his jaw but kept his Glock aimed at Randy.

CHAPTER SIXTEEN

Matt

"WELL, WELL, WELL," Randy said, grinning like a maniac, "What do we have here?" He wasn't wearing a ball cap this time, which made the tattoo covering his bald head clearly visible—an intricate geometric design.

Ever since their run-in with Randy on the day they'd arrived in California, the memory of Randy and the complete helplessness Matt had felt brought a fury upon him like he'd never known before. Now, seeing the man who was behind it standing there, once again thwarting their plans, Matt saw red.

"What do you want?" Matt spit out.

Randy shifted his gaze to Matt, his eyebrows raised in apparent surprise that Matt wasn't groveling at Randy's feet. "Your nose looks better, but those black eyes..." He tsk-tsked as he shook his head. "Not a good look for you, my friend."

Matt had to remind himself to unclench his jaw, and when he felt Jessica slip her hand into his, he inhaled slowly through his nose in an attempt to calm himself. He didn't want to do something stupid that would put her in danger.

"Toss your guns this way," Randy said.

Matt wanted to resist, wanted to pull out his gun and shoot at Randy until his magazine was empty, but he knew that wouldn't end well. Not with a dozen guns trained on them. Still, he didn't move.

Randy shifted his aim, pointing his gun directly at Jessica. "I'd hate to shoot the pretty lady, but I will."

Jessica softly gasped.

Hate-filled adrenaline flooded Matt's veins, but he withdrew his gun and tossed it on the ground without hesitation. So did Jessica. Matt turned to look at Derrick.

Cords stood out on Derrick's neck, but he tossed his Glock toward Randy. Chris followed suit.

Randy holstered his weapon and nodded at his men. One man scooped up the discarded guns while two other men quickly searched Matt and the others, taking the knife Matt had on his hip. Randy's men stepped away.

"What do you want?" Derrick asked, echoing Matt's earlier question.

Randy turned to Derrick, his head tilted. "Why do you think it's okay to take what belongs to me?"

What was he talking about? There was no way this RV dealership belonged to him. Randy was a gang-banger, not a businessman.

Derrick narrowed his eyes. "We haven't taken anything that belongs to you."

Matt couldn't help himself. "It's the other way around. You've taken things that belong to us."

A smile broke out across Randy's lips as he stared right at Matt. "You mean that sweet rig you paid in taxes?" His smile grew. "I especially appreciate that auxiliary fuel tank on *my* truck." He closed his eyes. "I hardly ever have to track down fuel now."

Anger burned in Matt's gut, but he kept himself under control. Barely.

"And that fifth wheel," Randy went on, a blissful smile lighting his face. "So comfortable. Especially that bed." His gaze slid to Jessica. "I know you used to sleep there." He inhaled deeply. "I smell your scent on my pillow every night." He touched his throat as his lips parted. "You fill my thoughts whenever my head touches that pillow." Randy's gaze slowly raked up and down Jessica's body as his tongue slowly slid along his lower lip. "Perhaps you'd like to join me one night."

Matt barreled toward Randy, his only thought to slam his fist into Randy's mouth to wipe that disgusting grin off of his face. Instead, before he reached the scumbag, he heard the blast of a gun as an excruciating pain tore through his upper thigh. He crashed to the asphalt, his leg feeling like it was on fire.

"Matt!" Jessica screamed as she raced to his side. "Oh, Matt." She lifted her gaze to Randy. "You shot him, you evil lowlife! You shot him!" Tears streamed down her face as she turned her attention to Matt, tearing off the sweatshirt she'd been wearing and tying it around his leg. "It'll be okay, baby. It'll be okay."

"For the record," Randy said, his voice soft and calm, "I didn't shoot your husband. One of my men did."

Matt didn't care who had pulled the trigger. It was an Emperor who had done it. Matt had been unarmed. There'd been no reason to shoot.

"Besides," Randy went on, "you should be grateful we only shot him in the leg."

Despite the pain, Matt actually was grateful. And rather surprised that they hadn't killed him. It had been idiotic to rush him. What had he thought they would do?

"Can you stand?" Jessica asked him.

Dizzy with pain, Matt wasn't ready to stand just yet. "Give me a minute."

Jessica nodded, then she turned to Derrick. "We need to go."

CHAPTER SEVENTEEN

Derrick

HATRED FOR RANDY and his crew scorched Derrick to his very soul. Even so, he had to maintain control. "As you can see, we have an injured man. We need to leave."

Randy chuckled. "Go right ahead."

Derrick knew it wouldn't be that easy. There was a reason Randy had shown up. In fact, Derrick would bet that one of the Emperors had been watching them the whole time and had alerted Randy that they were there. That had been why he'd felt they were being watched. Because they had been.

Knowing Randy wanted something, Derrick played along, going over to Matt and helping him slowly get to his feet. Chris joined him, standing on Matt's other side. Jessica stood back to let Derrick and Chris take Matt's weight between them as they hobbled toward the passenger side of Frank's truck. Jessica opened the door and they helped Matt get inside.

Expecting Randy to stop them at any moment, Derrick resisted the urge to look his way, instead focusing on making sure Jessica got safely behind the wheel of Frank's truck.

"Drive forward," he murmured to her. "Head to the exit and don't stop. But if you notice anyone following you, don't go back to the farm."

She nodded. "Wait. What about you and Chris?"

"We'll be right behind you." *Hopefully*. Derrick glanced at Chris, who stood nearby, rubbing the back of his neck, his lips tight. Derrick couldn't begin to imagine how Chris felt. He had a wife and two small children depending on him, but Derrick could read in Chris's body language that he wanted to take these guys out as much as Derrick did. That he was just holding himself in check. Derrick had no doubt that if he made a move, Chris would follow. A stony smile tugged at his lips.

"See you back at the farm," Jessica said, drawing Derrick's attention back to her.

He nodded, watching as she drove off, and as she left the dealership lot, he felt a sense of great relief. He didn't see anyone following her, but that didn't mean someone wasn't parked around the corner ready to tail her once she appeared. Hopefully she or Matt would notice if that happened.

"See what a generous emperor I am?" Randy asked.

Shooting one of his "subjects" didn't seem particularly generous to Derrick, but he wasn't about to point that out.

Why cause friction when they might be able to leave without further incident? Although Derrick was pissed that Randy had taken his Glock 21—his favorite weapon.

"Yeah," Derrick said as he and Chris strode past Randy and toward their truck and SUV, ready to get the heck out of there.

"Hold up," Randy said.

Prepared to ignore him, when Derrick saw several guns shift to follow him, he decided it would be a good idea to see what Randy wanted. He stopped beside the hood of his truck. Chris was right beside him.

"I hate this guy," Chris muttered only loud enough for Derrick to hear.

"You and me both," Derrick said in a low tone. As much as Derrick would have loved to wipe out Randy and every one of his men, that was unrealistic. He and Chris were outmanned and unarmed.

Derrick turned around and stared at Randy. "What is it?"

"What makes you think you can drive off with another one of my trailers?"

Derrick's eyebrows shot up. Randy was claiming all the RVs as his? Why did that not surprise him? "*Your* trailers?"

Randy swept his arms outward. "This *is* part of my kingdom. Everything within my kingdom belongs to me."

Which begged the question, Why did Randy let Matt and Jessica take the trailer that had been attached to Frank's truck? "I disagree."

Randy burst out laughing. "You say that as if your opinion

matters." He sobered, his eyes cold. "It doesn't." He paused. "You need to pay for the trailer your friend took."

I knew it! As furious as Randy's attitude made him, Derrick knew he was not in a position to fight him on it. "You never said anything about a payment when my friends left."

One side of Randy's mouth tilted up in the semblance of a smile. "They were in a big hurry. I didn't want to slow them down."

Right. Shaking his head in frustration, Derrick glanced at Chris, who sighed heavily.

"What do we owe you?" Chris asked.

Randy shifted his gaze to Chris. "I like that. Right down to business." He frowned toward Derrick. "And he didn't even argue." He smiled at Chris. "You're the one I'll deal with."

Randy's gaze slid over both the SUV and Derrick's truck and their attached trailers before going back to Chris. "You can keep the trailer your friends took." A menacing smile curved his lips. "To pay for it, I'll keep your truck and SUV."

Fury, hot and bright, ignited within Derrick. Pounding began in his ears as adrenaline rushed through his body. Now he knew how Matt had felt when Randy had stolen his truck and fifth wheel. Like he wanted to kill the man. Slowly.

Derrick's hands curled into fists at his side. Then he remembered the way Randy's man had shot Matt like he was a pesky fly. Was risking getting shot—and possibly killed—a price he was willing to pay to keep from losing his truck? No.

Breathe, damn it, breathe.

Using all the self-discipline he possessed, Derrick

managed to calm himself enough to keep from doing something he would regret. Silently counting to ten, he felt his pounding heart slow. Maybe he could reason with this lunatic. "We'll unhitch both trailers and then we'll go."

Randy's eyebrows tugged together. "Why would you unhitch the trailers?" Then he grinned as his expression smoothed out. "You want to keep your truck." He paused. "I get it."

Damn right he did. It wasn't just the truck, it was the principle of the thing.

Slowly shaking his head, Randy said, "Shoulda thought of that before helping yourself to something that's not yours."

Derrick couldn't stop himself. "You mean like you do?"

Randy stared hard at Derrick, then he burst out laughing and looked at his men, who also started laughing. After a moment, he sobered. "You're forgetting your place. *I* am Emperor Randy." He swept his hands outward. "This is *my* kingdom. I do what I please." Hands falling to his sides, he continued smiling. "*You* are nobody. *You* don't matter." He glanced at Chris. "None of your people do." His looked at Derrick with narrowed eyes. "I hope your friend dies."

It would have been easy to allow himself to become enraged, but Derrick forced himself to remain calm. Randy was just a nutjob trying to impress his men. Only problem was, his arrogance was affecting Derrick and his friends.

Derrick kept his expression neutral as he stared back.

"On your knees," Randy said, his voice laced with anger as he unholstered his gun and pointed it at Derrick.

Guess he hadn't gotten the rise out of Derrick that he'd expected. Maybe he'd been hoping Derrick would rush him like Matt had so he would have an excuse to shoot him.

Despite being fed up with Randy's bullying ways, Derrick didn't want to get shot, so he slowly knelt on the asphalt. Chris knelt beside him.

"Hands on your heads," Randy yelled.

Moving slowly, Derrick did as commanded.

Randy stalked over to him and pressed the gun against his temple.

Briefly closing his eyes at the feel of the cold steel against his skin, when Derrick opened them, he stared into Randy's dead eyes. No soul, just like Matt had said.

"I should shoot you right now," Randy murmured.

Though his heart was pounding, Derrick kept his eyes locked on Randy's.

A slow smile lifted the corners of Randy's lips and he pulled the gun away before taking a step back and turning to one of his men. "Bring me a revolver."

A moment later a man handed a revolver to Randy. With growing trepidation, Derrick watched as Randy opened the revolver's cylinder and dumped the bullets into his hand. He pocketed all but one bullet, dropping that one into the cylinder before spinning the cylinder and snapping it back into place.

With a wicked grin, Randy pressed the gun against Derrick's head just above his left ear. "Let's play a game."

Derrick didn't say a word.

"Where are you and your people staying?"

Derrick had been in a lot of dangerous situations when he'd been deployed in the Middle East, but he'd never had anyone play Russian Roulette with him. Still, he wasn't about to tell Randy a damn thing. Pressing his lips into a flat line, Derrick glared at him.

Randy pulled the trigger.

When Derrick heard the empty click, the thrum of near-death zinged through his body. Not a pleasant sensation.

Randy spun the cylinder, then pressed the gun to Derrick's temple. "Let's try that again." His voice was dangerously soft.

Derrick continued to glare. "Go to hell."

Crazed excitement burned in Randy's eyes. He pulled the trigger again.

Click.

How long was Randy going to play this game? Until Derrick was dead?

Randy spun the cylinder.

CHAPTER EIGHTEEN

Derrick

JUST AS DERRICK was wondering how long his luck would last, an explosion shattered the air and he was thrown to the ground.

Stunned, it took him several moments to regain his equilibrium, but he immediately knew this was his chance to take out Randy and his Emperors. Shaking off the light-headedness that swept over him, he forced himself to get to his feet. Once standing, he sought out Randy but didn't see his tattooed bald head anywhere. His men must have gotten him out of there. But they'd left behind half a dozen Emperors who were still splayed out on the ground.

Derrick glanced to his left where Chris was lying face down on the pavement. Chris lifted his head and gave it a shake. Confident that Chris was all right, Derrick turned his attention to the Emperors who were closest to him. He needed to get his hands on a gun. His own, if possible. But he'd take anything at this point. And where had the explosion come from? Was it a rival gang or friendlies? It was too soon for it to be his own group. There was no way Matt and Jessica could have gotten back and rallied the troops to come to their rescue.

Putting aside his questions, he focused on taking advantage of the distraction. Needing a weapon, Derrick lunged toward the nearest man and snatched his handgun from the pavement. Straightening, Derrick dropped the magazine, made sure it was full, and slammed it home. Then he pulled the slide to see if a bullet was in the chamber. One was. Without hesitation, he shot the man in the head. He went to the next man, who was beginning to move, and took him out, grabbing that man's gun and tossing it to Chris, who was now on his feet. Working together, they took out all the gang bangers who had been left behind.

Skirting around the RVs, Derrick and Chris cleared the dealership, ending in the area where the explosion had originated—a propane tank on the back of the lot.

"Did someone set that off?" Derrick asked, his gaze roving the area as he looked for anyone lurking about. "Or do you think the tank was leaking and exploded on its own?"

Chris shook his head. "No clue."

Derrick was mighty curious to know the answer. Because if someone had blown up the propane tank on purpose, he wanted to know if they'd meant to help Derrick and Chris or if it had just been a lucky coincidence. "Time to go."

"I agree. No telling if the Emperors will come back."

Absolutely. That was the last thing they needed. He and Chris hustled back to their vehicles. "Keep an eye out for a tail."

Chris grinned. "You got it."

Before they left, they collected all the weapons the Emperors had left behind. Much to Derrick's disappointment, his Glock 21 was not among them.

On the way back to the farm, Derrick turned on random streets to make sure no one was following them. Chris stayed right on his tail. When Derrick reached the farm's driveway, he saw Jeff standing guard. He waited while Jeff backed the box truck out of the way and opened the gate. Derrick drove through and Chris followed. Derrick saw Frank's truck with the trailer still attached to it. Good. Matt and Jessica had made it back.

Derrick and Chris parked their vehicles near Frank's truck, then they trotted over to Jeff, who had closed and locked the gate before blocking the driveway with the box truck.

"How's Matt?" Derrick asked Jeff as the three of them walked toward the house.

"Feeling like crap, but he'll be okay. Sarah fixed him up."

"Good to hear."

Jeff looked in the direction of the three trailers. "Kind of surprised you got 'em." He glanced at Derrick and Chris. "Jessica said the Emperors showed up."

Derrick replayed what had happened after Matt and

Jessica had left.

"An explosion?"

Derrick nodded. "Yep. No idea if it was on purpose or not."

"Huh."

When they reached the front porch, Derrick looked over the front of the property and toward the driveway. "We ought to camouflage the entrance. It's not real noticeable unless you know where to turn, but let's make it even harder to see."

Jeff nodded. "Sounds good to me."

The three of them gathered brush and put it in a pile. While they were working, Frank came out to see what they were doing. After they explained, he suggested attaching the brush to chicken wire he had in his barn.

They worked together to create two blinds, then dragged them past the box truck and through the gate, which Frank had opened. They attached the blinds to the gate, which would camouflage it while at the same time make it easy to open and close without having to move the blinds each time.

Derrick went through the gate, closing it behind him, then strode out onto the empty road, walking backwards for a distance before jogging forward. A vehicle would be driving a lot faster than he was jogging, but unless the driver knew where the entrance was, it would be easy to drive right past it.

Grinning, Derrick went back to the gate and went through, walking over to Frank, Jeff, and Chris. "It'll work."

They nodded and smiled, pleased with their efforts.

Frank shaded his eyes as he looked toward the trailers.

"Let's find a spot for those trailers."

Feeling good that despite the Emperors showing up they'd managed to get three trailers, Derrick walked with the other men toward the vehicles.

"Anyone thirsty?" Jessica asked as she, Emily, Amy, and Paisley came out of the house carrying glasses of water.

"Thanks," Derrick said. He took a glass from Paisley and downed it in one long gulp. The cool water refreshed him. He smiled at Paisley. "Where's your daughter?" She usually had the little girl right with her.

Paisley smiled in return. "Brooke and Kayla are playing with her."

Derrick took a moment to study Paisley. She was a tiny thing—couldn't be over five feet two inches. Her long blonde hair was up in a ponytail, emphasizing the soft curve of her jaw and her full lips. Her green eyes sparkled, drawing Derrick in.

When they'd rescued Paisley and her daughter from the side of the road, Derrick had been reluctant to let them come with their group. He knew now that he'd been wrong. She worked as hard as anyone else from their group. Harder than some. Now that he thought about it, every time he saw her she was engaged in some activity to keep the farm running.

Startled that he'd noticed so much about her, he tore his gaze away from her and turned to Jessica. "How's Matt doing?"

Jessica's eyebrows tugged together. "He's in a lot of pain, but Sarah's taking good care of him."

Anger at Randy and his gang stormed through Derrick. Then he remembered that he and Chris had dispatched six of Randy's men. That was six fewer men to hurt innocent people. He just wished they knew where the Emperors' base was so they could get rid of all of them like the vermin they were.

"Does Sarah need us to find anything for Matt?" Derrick asked. "Like antibiotics?"

"There's enough from what we got on our way out here, so we're good there."

Derrick thought about their experience on the road and the small gang that had taken over the pharmacy, extorting people in exchange for desperately needed medicine. Why did some people think it was okay to prey on others? It infuriated him.

"That's good news, at least," he said.

"Do you need help parking the trailers?" Jessica smiled. "I always helped Matt park the fifth wheel, although sometimes we ended up annoyed with each other."

Derrick chuckled.

Amy put an arm around Chris's waist. "It will be nice to have our own space." Then she looked at Frank as a blush climbed her cheeks. "I mean, we really appreciate your hospitality, but the boys can get a little...rambunctious."

Frank laughed. "I understand. And we're glad you're here."

Amy smiled softly. "Thank you."

"I was wondering," Paisley began, drawing everyone's attention to her, "who will be using the trailers?"

Derrick couldn't stop his gaze from sliding over her.

Annoyed with himself for being attracted to her, he knew he had to crush that right away. Things were too uncertain, too tense.

"Matt and I will use that one," Jessica said, pointing to the trailer attached to Frank's truck. "The other two are for Chris and Amy and you and Serena."

Paisley's forehead creased as she looked at each person. "Are you sure?" Her gaze went to Derrick. "What about you? Don't you want your own space?"

Those eyes. They seemed to see right into him. Distracted for a moment, when he realized he was staring, he tore his gaze away from her and looked at the trailers. "No, I'm good. I mean, I'll get something later."

"Okay. Thank you. I...I really appreciate it."

Refusing to look at her again, Derrick took a step toward the vehicles and trailers. "Let's get these bad boys parked."

"I'll keep watch," Jeff offered as he trotted off.

Working together, the group got all three trailers positioned and leveled. It took some time, but when they were done, Derrick thought it didn't look half bad.

"Where are the keys?" Frank asked.

Frowning, Derrick said, "We don't have them."

Frank's eyebrows shot up. "That'll make it a little harder to get inside, but not impossible."

Before they had a chance to do anything about it, Derrick heard Jeff shouting near the fence line, "Hold it right there! Hands where I can see them."

CHAPTER NINETEEN

Derrick

WITHOUT THINKING TWICE, Derrick drew his weapon—one of the guns he'd taken from the dead Emperors at the RV dealership. Holding it in the low ready position, he swiveled toward the area where Jeff stood and scanned the fence line. Chris, Frank, Emily, and Jessica were right beside him, their weapons drawn as well.

"Do you see anything?" Chris asked Derrick, his voice soft.

Squinting in the direction of the fence line, when Derrick saw movement, he said, "There. To the right of Jeff. Four men."

Now that he had his targets in view, Derrick marched forward, his gun pointed at the intruders. Chris was by his side and the others were on his flank.

The men had stopped just on the other side of the fence, their hands in the air.

"I'm Walter's son-in-law," one of the men shouted.

Derrick flashed back to the man who had shown up on the night they'd arrived, pleading for help to get his grandchildren back from the Emperors. Were these men legit?

"Where's Walter?" Jeff asked.

Derrick reached Jeff's side. The men were about twenty yards away.

"Home. He got hurt earlier."

"How did he get hurt?"

"Got a little too close to a flame."

Were they the ones who had blown up the propane tank? "Where did this happen?"

The man grinned. "You were there. At the RV dealership."

So, they were involved in the explosion. Still, how did he know this guy was actually Walter's son-in-law and not Emperors who had somehow found their group and were bent on revenge for Derrick and Chris killing six of their men? "How do we know you are who you say you are?"

The men were quiet a moment, then the one who said he was Walter's son-in-law said, "Walter came over a little over a week ago. Guess it was the night you guys got here. Said he asked you to help him get my kids back. You said no."

Guilt swept over Derrick, but he tamped it down.

It was extremely unlikely the Emperors would know that info. These guys were legit. Still pointing his gun at the men, Derrick nodded. "Put your hands down and come over."

"Would you mind lowering your weapons?" one of the men asked as they let their arms fall to their sides.

"I'm sure you understand why I can't. I don't know you."

"We saved your butts today."

Derrick thought it over. If those men hadn't set off that explosion, who knew what would have happened? He lowered his weapon but didn't holster it. Jeff and the others did the same.

The men crossed the fence and approached them. They had guns on their hips, but with their friendly smiles and relaxed bodies, Derrick didn't think they were a threat. The four men stopped in front of Derrick and Jeff, glancing at the people arrayed behind Derrick.

The one who said he was Walter's son-in-law looked Derrick in the eye. "I'm Jack Andrews." He pointed to the other men. "This is Scott, Charlie, and Ben."

Derrick nodded at them but didn't extend his hand. The virus could still be a risk. He wasn't going to take a chance. He did holster his weapon though. The others in his group followed his lead.

"Thanks for earlier," Derrick said, "at the dealership."

One side of Jack's mouth quirked up. "It was definitely our pleasure."

Still kind of flabbergasted that Jack had been there at just the right time, Derrick tilted his head as his eyebrows tugged together. "How'd you end up being there right when we needed you?"

Jack chuckled. "It wasn't planned that way, obviously."

"Right."

"Ever since the Emperors took my kids..." Jack swallowed before clearing his throat.

Talking to this man face to face and seeing how devastated he was by what had happened to him because of the Emperors only fueled Derrick's hatred of the group.

"Anyway," Jack said, "I've been trying to find where the Emperors' home base is. We were out on a scavenging run when we saw a parade of cars go by. The only time I ever see that many cars at once is when the Emperors are around, so it was a no brainer to follow them. I was hoping they'd lead us right to Mark and Ella."

Jack paused another moment before frowning. "When they stopped at that RV dealership, I'd hoped we'd finally found my children. We parked a distance away and crept up to check things out. That's when we saw you and the others." He glanced at Jessica and Chris. "Walter recognized you all right away, and when one of Randy's men shot your friend, we knew we needed to intervene."

Wow. They'd had no idea they were being observed. Of course, they'd been kind of busy dealing with Randy and his gang. Derrick was just glad it was the good guys who'd been there watching them.

"Walter figured there would be a propane tank on the lot," Jack said, "and he was right." A harsh smile lifted his lips. "We took advantage of the opportunity it presented."

Something occurred to Derrick. "How did you know the explosion wouldn't kill me or Chris?"

Jack's smile wavered. "We didn't, but it was a chance we had to take. Also, Walter thought the tank was far enough away from you so that it wouldn't kill you."

Smirking, Derrick said, "No. Only ring my bell."

"See? Walter was right. You're not dead."

That brought a round of laughter from everyone.

Derrick sobered. "We did manage to take out six of Randy's men."

Jack's eyebrows went up. "Nice."

Remembering how he and Chris hadn't seen anyone around shortly after the explosion, Derrick asked, "You took off pretty fast."

A smile slowly curved Jack's lips as he nodded. "That's because when Randy and his crew fled, we followed them." He paused dramatically. "Right to their lair."

That got Derrick's attention. His heart began to pound with anticipation. "You found their hideout?"

Jack's chin lifted as his shoulders went back. "Yep."

"Nice."

Jeff grinned. "Sweet."

"That's why we're here," Jack added. "We need more people before we rescue my kids." Jack paused a beat. "And take out Randy."

Derrick liked where this conversation was headed. Randy and his men needed to be stopped. Permanently.

Derrick didn't even check with the others in his group. He didn't have to. He knew how they felt. "We're in."

CHAPTER TWENTY

Derrick

"HOW MANY PEOPLE DO YOU HAVE?" Derrick asked Jack. Frank had led the group around back to the covered patio to discuss their plans in more detail.

Jack's lips tilted downward like he was less than happy about his answer. Then he swept his arms outward toward the three men that were with him. "You're looking at it."

Great.

Jack must have read the disappointment in Derrick's expression because he said, "That's why Walter asked for your help. We can't do it on our own."

No kidding.

But would Jack and his men plus Derrick, Jeff, Chris, and Frank be enough?

"So," Derrick said, "that gives us eight."

"Wait a second," Jessica said, her eyebrows forming an angry V. "You're completely ignoring the rest of us." She motioned to Emily, Amy, and Paisley. Then, after the briefest of hesitations, she glanced at Dylan. "Those men shot my husband. I'm not going to sit here and let you all fight on my behalf." She lifted her chin. "I've been training with the rest of you and I'm actually a pretty good shot. I want to fight the Emperors too."

Rather surprised by the passion in her voice, Derrick was pleased. Although he was pretty sure Matt wouldn't want her to go. But they needed her. And anyone else who would help. He looked at each of the other women. Emily nodded with certainty. Amy bit her lip, but Paisley stared right at Derrick before nodding.

"I'm in," Dylan said before Derrick even looked his way.

Kayla and Brooke looked less certain.

That was fine. They needed to leave a few people behind to care for the little ones and keep watch.

So, they had twelve. That sounded better than eight.

Not able to hold back his grin, Derrick shifted his eyes to Jack, whose smile matched Derrick's.

"Now that that's settled," Derrick said, his mind going to the mission, "what can you tell us about the layout? How many armed people did you see?"

Jack described what he'd observed, ending with, "I counted four armed men. No telling how many were inside the building or away from headquarters."

And no telling how brutal those men would be. Still, the

Emperors wouldn't be expecting an attack. Derrick and the rest would have the element of surprise on their side. "I'd like to do a little recon myself."

"I'll go with you," Jeff immediately offered.

Glad to have him by his side, Derrick nodded.

Jack frowned. "I've already checked it out. We need to get there and get my kids. Today. Right now."

Though Derrick understood Jack's eagerness, there was no way he would risk the lives of his people without scoping out the place himself. Wasn't going to happen.

"We'll get your kids," he said, hoping to calm Jack down, "but you have to understand that I've done these kinds of missions before and I've learned that things will and do go wrong. We need to be prepared or we're going to end up with dead people." It was harsh and it was blunt, but it had to be said.

Jack shook his head ever so slightly, broadcasting annoyance. "Fine. But I don't want to wait a minute longer than necessary."

Neither did Derrick. The sooner the Emperors were dead, the better. "Agreed." Then he thought about all the bullets that would be flying. He wanted to do whatever he could to minimize casualties, but besides himself, Chris, and Jeff, no one had combat experience. "It sure would be nice if we had some body armor or vests."

Everyone nodded. After a moment of silence, Frank spoke up. "I know where we can get vests."

All eyes went to him.

"Not sure why I didn't think of this earlier," he said, his smile turning chagrined, "but there's a 5.11 Tactical store just a few miles from here. I know they have plate carrier vests and other gear."

Derrick grinned at Jeff, whose eyes had lit up. Derrick felt the same way. "We'll stop there first, then we'll do the recon."

"Anyone hungry?" Sarah asked as she came out of the house carrying a platter filled with sandwiches made with homemade bread, peanut butter, and homemade jam.

Now that she mentioned it, Derrick was famished. "Just a quick bite," he said, "then we'll go."

Jeff was on his feet and taking the platter from Sarah. "You don't have to ask me twice." He set the platter on the table and picked up a sandwich before taking a huge bite.

"Thank you," Jack said with a smile at Sarah as he took a sandwich.

Derrick wondered what Jack's food situation was but didn't ask. They had enough on their shoulders without worrying about the needs of other groups.

After everyone had gotten their share—not enough to fill them, but enough to keep them going until the next meal—Derrick, Jeff, Jack, and Jack's three men headed out. Jack and his men had parked outside of the farm's property, so the four of them walked out of the gate before getting into their SUV.

Derrick led the way in his truck with Jack and his crew behind them. First, they stopped at the 5.11 Tactical store, gearing up with tactical vests and other goodies, including breaching tools, holsters, chest rigs, and boots.

Like a kid in a candy store, Derrick could hardly contain his excitement, but he kept his cool as he stocked up on anything and everything he thought he and his group would need.

Loaded down, he and Jeff decided to drop their gear at the farm before doing recon. Finally, as he and Jeff followed Jack and his group to a stopping point about a mile from the Emperors' headquarters, he felt the soberness of the situation slide over him. The men they were about to observe were evil. They'd taken Jack's two children without a second thought and who knew how many others? He didn't want to think about what they were doing with them.

"There will be innocents among these wolves," Derrick said with a frown.

Jeff nodded. "Yeah. I was thinking the same thing. It's both a rescue mission and a take-down."

Jack pulled his SUV into a parking lot. Derrick followed, then he and Jeff got out of the truck and met up with the others.

"From here, it's half a mile," Jack said, his eyes broadcasting how hard it was for him to be so close to his children without being able to rescue them right that minute.

Derrick nodded. Then, when Jack set off at a jog through the lot and toward a long line of motionless trains, Derrick followed.

"Here's the best vantage point," Jack whispered as he hunkered down behind a train covered with graffiti.

Derrick squatted beside him and took a pair of binocs out

of the pack on his back, glassing the scene in front of him. It was a large warehouse with a chain-link fence surrounding the property. Three armed men were walking the perimeter, although Derrick noticed that of the three, only one seemed fully attentive. The others appeared to be bored, their eyes not scanning as sharply as the one guard's were.

Good. It would be easier to sneak up on guards who were only doing what they were told but obviously didn't think was necessary.

They watched the area for a while.

"I'm going to recon the other sides of the building," Derrick said. "I shouldn't be long."

Jeff raised his eyebrows like he was asking if Derrick wanted him to come along.

"It'll be quicker alone," Derrick said.

Jeff nodded once.

Staying in a low crouch, Derrick made his way to another building where he had good cover. He studied the Emperors' headquarters from that side before managing to get a good look at the last two sides, then he headed back to Jeff and the others.

"Well?" Jack asked, clearly ready to get this done.

Derrick grinned. "I have a plan."

They trotted back to where they'd left their vehicles, and then Derrick laid out his idea for attacking the Emperors. After a few suggestions and adjustments, everyone was in agreement. "We'll hit them at midnight after everyone is presumably asleep." He looked at Jack. "Meet at our place at eleven to gear up."

"Sounds good," Jack said, then he and his men left.

CHAPTER TWENTY-ONE

Jessica

JESSICA FELT LIKE A FRAUD. Yeah, she'd talked a good game about going with everyone and fighting the Emperors, but as she stood in the garage with everyone else and prepared the gear Derrick had given them, dread wormed its way through her, taking hold of her chest and squeezing so hard she had trouble breathing. She was a dental hygienist, for heaven's sake. Not a warrior. But she'd committed to going, and if she didn't do this right, she would end up dead.

Even worse was seeing Dylan in his gear ready to do battle. That made her mama's heart stutter with an unspeakable fear. Imagining something happening to her son brought hot tears springing into her eyes. Blinking frantically to clear her vision, she breathed slow and easy and forced her thoughts to the only acceptable outcome—success.

Derrick had a good plan and he was doing everything he

could to keep the less-experienced people out of harm's way while still making them a useful part of the team. She appreciated that, but bullets would still be hurtling toward her and Dylan. And everyone else.

Then there was Matt. He knew all about the battle. He just didn't know she was going. All evening she'd been avoiding telling him. But she had too. What if she didn't come home? She couldn't leave without saying good-bye.

Suppressing a sigh, she tucked a spare magazine into her tactical vest, grateful Derrick had gone on his shopping spree, then she set the vest aside and went into the house.

As she approached the room where Matt was resting—Jeff and Emily had temporarily switched spaces with her and Matt —she gathered her nerve and tried to come up with what to say, but when she walked into the room and saw him lying there, his bandaged leg propped up on a stack of pillows and his handsome face relaxed as he slept, the horror she'd felt only hours earlier as he'd been shot raced through her. The image of him falling to the ground, blood pooling around his leg, blasted into her mind. Matt had only been protecting her after Randy's disgusting suggestion. There had been no reason for the Emperors to shoot him. Matt had been unarmed. Even though it hadn't been a mortal wound, with no hospitals or medical care available, even a minor wound could be fatal. But Randy didn't care. He and his gang-bangers were an evil menace that needed to be stopped.

Rage and a need for revenge plowed through Jessica, shocking her into stillness as she stood beside the bed. She would go on this mission and she would do whatever it took to make sure the Emperors were no longer a threat to the safety of her family and friends.

She realized she was breathing heavily, so deep was her need to *do something.*

"Babe," Matt said as his eyes fluttered open and settled on her.

Jessica sat on the chair by the head of the bed and took Matt's hand. "Hey, sweetie. Do you need anything? Water? Something to eat?"

"Water would be great."

She released his hand and grabbed the cup on the bedside table before holding the straw to his lips. He took a few sips, then his head fell back against the pillow. "What's happening? Has everyone left for the Emperors' compound?"

Forcing a smile, she shook her head. "Not yet."

Matt's jaw clenched as he stared into the distance. "I want to go with them. So bad."

"I know, sweetheart. But there are plenty of people going."

He met her gaze. "Who's going?"

"Let's see." She looked up as she pictured the faces of everyone going. "Derrick and Jeff and Chris, of course." She glanced at Matt. "Frank's going, as well as Jack and his three buddies."

Matt nodded. "That's good."

Forcing herself to look him in the eye, she said, "Emily and Paisley are going too."

Matt's eyebrows shot up. "Really?"

"Uh-huh."

His eyes narrowed. "What aren't you telling me? Is Dylan going?"

At the look of concern in Matt's eyes, Jessica felt her heart compress with worry again. "Yeah."

Matt sighed. "We need everyone we can get. And in this world, Dylan's practically a man." Smiling grimly, he added, "I know Derrick will watch out for him."

She had to just say it. "I'll watch out for him too."

Matt looked at her sharply. "Wait. What are you saying?"

"I'm...I'm going too."

He jerked upward, then grimaced in pain as his face went white, forcing him to fall back against the pillow. "No, Jessica. No."

She took one of his hands in hers. "I love you, Matt, and I know you want me to stay on the farm and never leave, but I'm going. The more people we have, the better our chances for success."

His face tightened. "This isn't a food run, Jess, this is battle. Men wanting to *kill*." He stared at her, his gaze intense. "They will happily *murder* you, Jess." He swallowed several times. "Or worse."

He was right. She knew he was right. But that didn't change anything. She had to carry her weight, had to do her part. But first she had to convince Matt. Not that he could physically stop her, but she wanted—no, *needed*—his support.

"Dylan and Emily and Paisley and I are going to be in a

ditch. We're just going to deliver covering fire while the people with combat experience go in close."

"You realize that in the heat of battle the best plans never go as expected, right?"

That was one of her biggest fears, actually. "I know, which is why Derrick told us to fall back if things look like they're going south." Squeezing his hand, she smiled. "I promise I'll stay far away from danger."

Before he could argue anymore, she leaned in and kissed him. He wrapped his arms around her and held her tight. When she finally drew away, she reached out and stroked his face. Tears shimmered in his eyes, which brought tears to her own.

"I love you, Matt. I'll be back before you know it."

He slowly shook his head, his jaw clenched like he was barely holding himself together.

With a final smile, Jessica stood and left the room, not allowing herself to look back as tears clouded her eyes.

CHAPTER TWENTY-TWO

Derrick

"WE'LL HAVE to hoof it the rest of the way," Derrick said to the assembled group. They'd parked half a mile away from the perimeter of the Emperors' headquarters.

The sun had set long ago, and with everyone dressed in black, they were well camouflaged. Derrick swept his gaze over each and every person. Some, like Jeff and Chris, had their game faces on, ready for the mission. Others, like Paisley and Jessica, looked terrified, their eyes wide. The rest had varying looks of determination and fear etched in their faces.

His plan was sound. It would work. It had to.

"Our top priority is rescuing Jack's kids," he said, although he hoped he would be the one to come face to face with Randy. "Any questions?"

All heads shook in the negative.

With a single nod, he said, "Let's go."

They walked together until they reached the train yard, where they stopped.

"We all have to cross the ditch," Derrick said. He had mixed feelings about some of them being there and hoped the less-experienced among them wouldn't be needed at all, but if push came to shove, the more guns on their side, the better. They'd all been training. He was confident in their abilities.

They set off single file, reaching the ditch in just a few moments. All of them hunkered down as Derrick directed Jessica, Paisley, Emily, and Dylan where to position themselves. With the darkness and the high sides of the ditch, they were basically invisible.

Once those four were in place, Derrick and the rest of the team waited in the ditch until the guard within view had passed, then they sprinted to the fence line and used a pair of wire cutters to cut a man-sized opening in the chain-link fence. They poured through, dividing into four pairs before heading to their assigned areas. Jeff was with Derrick.

A large warehouse loomed in front of them, the glow of the moon casting enough light for them to see where they were going. Using hand signals, the pair communicated their intentions, silently approaching a guard who had stopped to smoke a joint. Jeff kept watch while Derrick crept up behind the man, slapping his hand over the man's mouth, then slitting his throat before he could react. The man's body went limp. Derrick held on to him, helping him noiselessly slump to the pavement.

On the lookout for any other Emperors, they advanced

toward the building. The rest of the teams were assigned to take out the remaining guards. Derrick hoped they hadn't had any trouble. He didn't hear any commotion, which was a good sign.

Derrick and Jeff waited by a corner of the building. A few minutes later Frank and Chris, as well as Jack and his three men—Ben, Scott, and Charlie—appeared. From the looks on their faces, they'd been successful in taking out all of the guards. Good.

The plan was to go inside and spread out, looking for Jack's kids while taking out as many Emperors as they could. Trouble was, none of them had any idea where the kids were —or if they were even there. Plus, it would be pitch black inside.

What Derrick wouldn't give for a pair of night vision goggles. No matter. They would deal with the situation as it was.

Everyone stood back as Chris reached for the door that led inside. Chris grabbed the handle and pulled the door open. Derrick and Jeff were right there, leading with their guns, ready to shoot anything that moved.

All was silent.

They went inside. Moonlight filtered in through the windows, allowing them to see that they were in a small reception area. A hallway to the right had several closed doors coming off of it while a closed door stood behind the reception counter. With a nod, the men broke into four teams of two men. One team—Jack and Charlie—went behind the counter to investigate what was behind that door while the other three teams headed down the hall. Using his flashlight sparingly, Derrick led the way. This area was obviously the office space. Each team took a door.

Working together, Derrick and Jeff silently entered one of the rooms. It was a conference room with a pair of windows, casting enough moonlight for Derrick to see that there were four men sleeping on cots. With a grim expression, Derrick slit two of the men's throats while Jeff took out the other two. They wouldn't use their guns unless it was absolutely necessary. The longer they had the advantage of surprise the better.

They left the room, meeting up with the other three teams, who nodded their success. Each held up two fingers. Ten men down. Good.

"Randy?" Derrick mouthed.

Everyone shook their heads in the negative.

That meant there had to be more than a few men yet to kill.

They continued down the hall, reaching another door. Derrick opened it. It was the main warehouse. Dim light glowed from one corner of the cavernous space, although the light came from behind tall shelves. Someone was up and about, but Derrick couldn't see anyone. The area directly around them was thick with darkness.

Cautiously entering the space, Derrick kept his head on a swivel. The rest of the men followed. Once the eight of them were inside, Frank silently closed the door. They spread out, ready to swarm the place and take out whoever they could.

That's when all hell broke loose.

"Intruders!" someone shouted.

Gunshots rang out. Derrick dove to the ground, but he heard one of his men grunting. Someone had been hit. It was too dark to see who it was. Grabbing the string of firecrackers from his vest, Derrick lit the fuse and threw them off in the distance.

Bang bang bang!

The noise added to the confusion, but it drew the gunfire of the enemy away from Derrick and his men long enough for them to scramble to safety behind a tall shelving unit. When they got there, Derrick swept his gaze over everyone, which was when he realized Ben was missing. Frantically looking to the others, he saw Jack shake his head. Ben was dead. They'd just made contact with the enemy that was awake and already they'd lost a man.

Shoving down his concern, Derrick motioned instructions. The pop of the firecrackers was slowing down. Time was running out. Derrick, Chris, and Frank went toward the gunshots that were still echoing while the other four headed the other way, preparing to flank the enemy.

Marching forward with his gun at the ready, when Derrick caught sight of a pair of Emperors through the shelving, he stopped and took aim. Beside him, Chris aimed as well. With a nod, they shot at the same time, dropping both men. Frank had his back to Derrick and Chris, watching their rear.

With the little bit of light, Derrick could see well enough to move forward. Gunshots rang out in another part of the warehouse. He hoped it was his men shooting and not the Emperors.

A staircase came into sight. It led to a landing with an office that had windows overlooking the warehouse. Is that where Randy was? Derrick peered upward, but it was completely dark inside the office. With a shake of his head, he pressed forward, determined to clear the main warehouse before attempting to ascend the stairs.

CHAPTER TWENTY-THREE

Jessica

JESSICA COULD HEAR gunshot after gunshot from inside the warehouse. What was happening? Should they go in and help? Should they fall back? What if Derrick and the others were shot? The Emperors would come outside and find her and the others. Of course they would. It would only make sense for them to search the surrounding area. She and Dylan and Paisley and Emily would be killed. Or worse.

Jessica looked toward Emily, but she was too far away and it was too dark. Desperate to know what to do, she had to force herself not to call out.

Someone burst through the door of the warehouse, running flat-out in their direction.

Straining to see if it was one of her people, Jessica lifted her handgun, her hands shaking as she aimed. It was a man. She could tell that much. He paused at the hole in the chain-link fence, then he climbed through before running again. He was headed straight for them. That meant it had to be one of their people, right?

Terrified to shoot the wrong person, but also terrified for one of the Emperors to find them, she froze, her gaze riveted on the person who was getting closer, closer.

He changed directions slightly. Now he was headed toward Dylan. Taking a quick glance in Dylan's direction, Jessica saw her fourteen-year-old son holding his ground as he stood in the ditch, standing straight and tall, his gun pointed at the man, his head and shoulders above the edge of the ditch.

She shifted her gaze to the man. He was fifty feet away. She didn't recognize him. Was he one of Jack's men? He was getting closer—thirty feet, twenty feet. No, she'd never seen him before.

Dylan's gun went off. Jessica gasped. His shot missed. Ten feet from Dylan, the man halted and lifted his gun, pointing it right at Dylan. Jessica didn't hesitate. She sighted in on the man and pulled the trigger. Once, twice. The man fell and didn't move.

She'd killed him. He was dead. Shockwaves crashed over her. She'd taken a life.

But she'd saved Dylan's. A sigh rattled from her chest.

Another gunshot sounded. This one close by. A body crumpled not far from the ditch. Who'd shot him? Emily?

Other Emperors could be out there, trying to escape the

mayhem inside. Jessica turned her attention to her surroundings. Nothing moved.

When it was silent for a dozen heartbeats, she whispered, "Is everyone all right?"

"Yeah," someone whispered back, but she couldn't tell if it was Emily or Paisley. She could see that Dylan was okay.

"I'm good," another voice answered.

Okay. All four of her group were safe and sound.

Exhaling in relief, when she heard more gunshots coming from inside the warehouse, the brief calm she'd felt fled. Not knowing what was happening was the worst part.

CHAPTER TWENTY-FOUR

Derrick

THEY'D TAKEN out every man in the main warehouse space. Time to climb those stairs and see what was behind door number one.

With Jeff and Chris behind him, Derrick strode to the bottom of the stairs. He turned to them. "I'll go up alone. Watch my six."

They nodded. They knew the drill.

Derrick had taken three steps up when the door to the office swung open and Randy stepped onto the wide landing at the top of stairs. But he wasn't alone. He had a teenaged girl in front of him like a shield and he was holding a gun to her head.

Derrick pointed his gun at Randy's head.

"Ella!" Jack yelled as he sprinted across the floor of the warehouse and toward the stairs. When he reached the bottom, Jeff and Chris held him back. Good. He was too emotional and would only get in the way.

Derrick stared at Randy. Jack's appearance hadn't shaken him at all. The gun was still pressed to Ella's skull. Tears streamed down her face. Derrick had never met this girl, but he couldn't help but make the comparison to Kayla and Brooke, girls he cared about. And he knew what it felt like to have Randy press a gun to his head. Ella had to be panic-stricken.

"Let her go," Derrick demanded, his voice calm yet commanding.

Randy licked his lips then shook his head. "No. Drop your weapons and get off of the stairs. I'm getting out of here."

Not if Derrick had anything to do with it. "Your men are all dead. Time to give up."

Randy had to be nervous now that he didn't have his thugs to do his dirty work for him. He glared at Derrick. "I'll shoot her."

"No!" Jack screamed.

Ignoring Jack and keeping his gun steady on Randy, Derrick shook his head. "No, you won't. Because if you do, I'll kill you."

Randy's gaze bounced from place to place as if someone was going to appear and save him. "You're going to kill me anyway."

That was true, but Derrick wasn't going to admit it. "Let the girl go, Randy. Now."

He shook his head. "No. She's my insurance policy." His

eyes narrowed. "Get out of the way. Now." He pressed the gun harder into Ella's head. She let out a terrified scream.

"Get off the stairs, Derrick!" Jack yelled, "Or I'll shoot you myself."

Derrick knew Jeff and Chris were disarming Jack the moment he spoke those words, so Derrick didn't even acknowledge him. Instead, he kept his gaze steady on Randy. "If you let her go, I'll let you go." Bald-faced lie, but if it saved the girl, who cared? Randy didn't deserve to live.

Randy seemed to consider the offer, but he must have known Derrick was yanking his chain. "I don't believe you."

Well, he wasn't a complete idiot. Derrick shook his head. "No one else needs to die." *Except you.*

Randy tugged Ella's back tighter against his chest and moved the gun to under her chin.

Ella let out a petrified whimper.

"Please, Randy," Jack said, his voice nearly a sob. "I'll do anything. Just let her go."

Randy's eyes shifted to Jack, his expression changing back to the Randy Derrick had grown to hate. Jack's weakness did something to Randy, made the evil in him blossom like a poisonous flower. It was clear on his face and in his dead eyes. "I think I'll shoot her anyway," Randy sneered at Jack, jamming the gun into Ella's chin all the harder.

"Daddy!" Ella sobbed.

"NO!" Jack screamed.

Time to put an end to this. "Knock it off, Randy. The moment you shoot her, I kill you."

Randy's eyes shifted to Derrick, the evil confidence he'd displayed mere seconds before beginning to slip. "I'll do it."

Derrick sighted in on Randy's head. "So will I." Derrick considered shooting Randy, but the risk of hitting Ella was too great. He wasn't prepared to sacrifice the girl just to get to Randy. He would get his chance to kill the weasel. He just had to be patient.

As he stared at Randy and Ella, Derrick thought he saw movement in the darkened window behind them. Was someone else in there? That would complicate things. But if it was one of Randy's men, why hadn't the man already opened fire?

Movement again. This time from behind Randy.

It was a kid. A teenaged boy. Was that Ella's brother —Mark?

Not allowing his eyes to stray to Mark—he didn't want to give away his presence—Derrick used his peripheral vision to track Mark's movements. But when he saw Mark lift a large object over his head, ready to bring it down on Randy, Derrick braced himself for the aftermath.

Crash!

Randy was completely taken by surprise as the object— looked like a lamp—hit him over the head. The gun flew from his hand, falling to the warehouse floor below, and as he jerked under the force, he shoved Ella, who tumbled forward. Derrick dashed up the stairs, catching Ella before she fell any farther, dropping his gun in the process.

Jeff and Chris must have released Jack, because moments

later he was there, wrapping Ella in his arms. Mark raced down the stairs to reunite with his father.

Not about to rest, not with Randy still breathing, Derrick took the remaining stairs two at a time, reaching the landing just as Randy began to sit up. The easy thing would have been to shoot him, but Derrick's gun was nowhere to be seen. Just as well. His fists were itching to connect with Randy's face.

Randy lifted his gaze to Derrick, the deadness in his eyes back in full force now that Derrick wasn't pointing a gun at him. Randy shook his head like he was shaking off a bit of dizziness, then he leapt to his feet.

A steely smile curved Derrick's lips as his hands curled into fists.

A menacing grin split Randy's face as he jabbed a knife toward Derrick.

Where had that come from? Nearly caught off guard, Derrick reacted on instinct, his left hand shooting out and pressing against Randy's bicep, keeping Randy from ramming the knife at him. He slid his hand down Randy's arm to his wrist, pushing Randy's wrist back and trapping the knife against Randy's thigh. Randy tried to free his hand, but Derrick held it tight, then he jammed his other forearm against Randy's throat and shoved him backwards until Randy's back hit the wall. While pressing his forearm into Randy's throat, Derrick squeezed Randy's wrist until the knife fell from his hand. Derrick kicked it. The knife clattered to the warehouse floor below.

Now that the knife was no longer a factor, Derrick

released Randy's wrist, curling his own hand into a fist before slamming it into Randy's right kidney. A muffled grunt escaped Randy's lips, but just barely because Derrick's forearm was cutting off his oxygen. That's when Randy began to fight back, both fists swinging wildly. One punch connected with Derrick's temple, surprising him and loosening his forearm against Randy's throat. Randy managed to shove Derrick back a few steps, then he drove forward, obviously ready to barrel into Derrick. Reading Randy's body language, Derrick stepped aside, then swept a leg behind one of Randy's ankles. Randy crashed to the floor, landing on his back. Before he had a chance to recover, Derrick was on him, a knee in his chest.

Randy struggled to get up but couldn't under Derrick's weight. As Derrick stared into Randy's furious eyes, he thought about all that Randy had done—taking vital supplies that didn't belong to him, stealing Jack's kids and doing who knew what with them, allowing his men to shoot Matt and then saying he hoped Matt would die, and then playing Russian Roulette on Derrick, the thrill of murder blazing in his eyes the entire time. Rage, hot and black, flooded Derrick. Randy was an evil, despicable lowlife who was a stain on society. A cancer that needed to be eliminated before he could hurt anyone else. And Derrick was the one who was going to make that happen.

Derrick grabbed his knife from the sheath at his back. Gripping the handle with one hand, he pressed the tip of the blade to the V at Randy's throat. Then, using his other hand, he slammed his palm against the handle, thrusting the blade deep into Randy's throat.

A look of stunned disbelief widened Randy's eyes, and then, after a brief moment, he stopped moving.

He was dead.

It wasn't triumph that settled over Derrick, but rather a grim satisfaction that the head of the snake had been cut off. The Emperors were no more.

CHAPTER TWENTY-FIVE

Derrick

SUDDENLY EXHAUSTED, Derrick stood over Randy and stared at him. So weak, so useless. Randy had had an army behind him. He could have made a difference. Instead, he'd chosen to terrorize and steal.

"Good riddance," Derrick muttered.

A commotion sounded inside the office as two women stumbled out, their eyes wide.

"Who... who are you?" one of them asked Derrick.

Derrick wasn't surprised to discover women stashed in the office along with Ella and Mark. Smiling gently, he said, "We're here to free you."

The woman who had asked burst into tears. The other looked like she was in shock.

He looked toward the office. "Are there any more people in there?"

The woman shook her head. "It was just us and the two kids."

Glad no one else had been terrorized, Derrick nodded before helping them down the stairs where Jeff, Chris, and Frank waited. Jack was huddled with his children while Scott and Charlie stood nearby.

"Can you take us home?" one of the women asked.

"I'll make sure you get home safely," Scott said, stepping forward.

Charlie nodded. "I will too."

Derrick scooped up his fallen weapon, then saw that the gun Randy had dropped was the Glock 21 Randy had stolen from him. Smiling, Derrick holstered it.

"Can I talk to you a minute?" Jack asked him.

Derrick turned and faced him. He wouldn't hold Jack's threats against him. He could only imagine what the man had been through. Still, he wouldn't necessarily trust him either.

"I, uh, I want you to know that I'm grateful for what you did." His eyes went to Frank, Jeff, and Chris, then back to Derrick. "All of you, helping me get my kids back."

Derrick nodded. "Sorry about the loss of your man."

Jack's jaw tightened. "Ben was a good man." He glanced toward Randy's body. "Ben's sacrifice wasn't for nothing."

"No. It wasn't."

"If your group needs anything, well, you know where we are."

Nodding, Derrick said, "Appreciate that."

"Hey," Jeff said, "Look at this."

Derrick turned to see what Jeff was talking about and saw Jeff's flashlight beam sweeping over the warehouse shelves near them. Cases of canned goods were stacked high, along with boxes of crackers and pasta and other supplies.

"Guess this is where they put the food they took from all of those houses," Chris said.

A smile slowly curved Derrick's lips. It would go a long way to helping their group survive. Then he remembered Jack and his group. He swiveled to face him. "What do you say we divide this up?"

Happiness lit Jack's face. "That's a great idea."

Derrick looked at the women they'd rescued. "We'll make sure you get some too."

They smiled. "Thank you."

Derrick turned to Jack. "We can divide the weapons too."

Jack nodded. "Sounds good to me."

"Before we load up," Chris said, "let's see if we can find where Randy kept all of those RV keys." He grinned. "Unless you want to pry open the trailer doors."

Smiling, Derrick said, "No. Keys would be nice."

With Chris leading the way, Derrick went up the stairs, past Randy's body, and into the office. It didn't take long to find a box filled with keys.

"This must be it," Chris said with a smirk.

"Nice."

Digging through the box, Chris shook his head. "We'll have to take all of 'em and figure out the right ones later."

That gave Derrick an idea, but first they needed to get

Jessica, Emily, Dylan, and Paisley. They hadn't had any contact with them. Derrick hoped they'd made it through the battle unscathed. With Chris, Jeff, and Frank by his side, Derrick walked out of the warehouse and into the night. As the four of them got closer to the ditch, Derrick saw a body sprawled out. Alarmed that gunfire had been exchanged, he was surprised when his thoughts first went to Paisley.

"Jeff!" Emily shouted as she vaulted out of the ditch and raced into Jeff's arms.

Moments later the other three climbed out of the ditch and hurried toward them. To Derrick's great relief, they looked unharmed. "Everyone okay?" he asked, his eyes going to Paisley.

"We're fine," Jessica said, drawing Derrick's attention to her.

"Good."

"What happened in there?" Jessica asked. "We heard so many gunshots."

"Randy's dead."

Jessica's eyebrows shot up. "Really? You're sure?"

Chuckling softly, Derrick nodded. "I'm sure."

"What about the rest of them?" Dylan asked.

Derrick turned to him. "All the Emperors who were here are dead." He glanced at the nearby body. "Looks like you guys took out an Emperor too."

"My mom did it," Dylan said with a proud smile.

This raised Derrick's eyebrows.

Jessica bit her lip like she was worried she would be judged. "He was going to shoot Dylan."

Derrick thought about how many Emperors he'd killed that night. "No need for an explanation."

Jessica smiled softly, then nodded.

Emily put an arm around Paisley. "Paisley shot one too."

This surprised Derrick even more, and when he looked at the petite woman he appraised her once again. "That right?"

She met his gaze and lifted her chin. "Yeah. And I'd do it again."

Proud of her mental strength, Derrick had to tear his eyes away.

"Did you find Jack's kids?" Jessica asked, her voice showing deep concern.

Glad he had good news, he nodded. "Yeah. They're safe and sound."

She released a huge breath. "Oh, thank goodness."

He considered not telling them that Ben had been killed, but decided they deserved to know. "Jack lost one of his men. Ben."

"Oh no," Jessica said.

Ready to turn the conversation to something happy, Derrick gestured to the box Chris held. "Found the keys to the trailers."

Chris laughed. "At least we hope the keys we need are in here."

Smiling, Derrick added, "We also found a good stash of food. We'll get our vehicles and load it up." He turned to

Jessica. "Before we head home, I want see if your truck's here. If it is, we can surprise Matt."

Her eyebrows shot up. "That would be awesome." Her lips curved in a hope-filled smile. "And maybe our fifth wheel's here too."

Tilting his head, Derrick said, "Maybe." He didn't want to get her hopes up, but when he'd done his recon he'd seen an RV that looked suspiciously like Matt and Jessica's.

Smiling broadly, Jessica asked, "What are we waiting for?"

The group went into a slow jog. Derrick kept an eye out for any Emperors who might show up unexpectedly. Before long, they reached their vehicles, which they drove up to the warehouse. Once the food and other supplies were loaded, Derrick led the group to the area where he'd seen the RV.

"That's it!" Jessica said as a truck and RV came into view, her voice filled with excitement. "Matt will be so happy."

"Do you know how to hitch it?" Derrick had never hitched a fifth-wheel to a truck before and he didn't want his first attempt to be in the middle of the night when the light was less than good.

She grimaced. "Uh, no. I usually assist while Matt does the backing up."

"I can do it," Frank said with a grin.

A short time later the RV was hitched to Matt and Jessica's truck.

Jessica smiled at Derrick. "Looks like you can have the extra trailer now."

That hadn't occurred to him, but he had to admit that it

would be nice to have some space to himself. He was used to living alone, after all. Being around everyone 24/7 had been a challenge. "Nice."

Jeff was looking around and Derrick realized he was trying to find his truck and trailer, which Randy had taken the day they'd arrived.

"Any luck?" he asked him.

Jeff scowled. "Nope. The idiot probably wrecked it."

"Sorry, man."

Jeff just shook his head.

As they drove back to the farm, Derrick relished the thrill of victory and tried not to worry about what other obstacles they would inevitably face.

CHAPTER TWENTY-SIX

Derrick

DERRICK HAD FINALLY GOTTEN a good night's sleep. Knowing the Emperors were no more did that to him. It also didn't hurt that he finally had his own space. Once they'd gotten back from their battle, they'd taken the time to find keys for all three trailers among the mass of keys in the box and now he was sitting on the couch in his new home. In a few minutes he was going to join everyone in surprising Matt with his truck and RV. It had been Jessica's idea and everyone was looking forward to this bright spot. Matt had been awake when they'd gotten back—he'd told them there was no way he could sleep knowing Jessica and Dylan were out there. But he'd been in the bedroom and hadn't seen them pull in with his truck and RV.

A knock sounded on Derrick's door. Jumping to his feet, Derrick smiled, expecting it to be Jeff or Chris, but when he saw Paisley standing there with Serena on her hip, he was taken aback.

She was smiling brightly. "Everyone's ready."

He felt like an idiot as he stared at her dumbly. Finally, he said, "Okay. Great."

She turned and walked away without another word. Clearly, she had no attraction to him. Surprised at the disappointment that shot through him, he climbed down the steps of his trailer and headed into the house.

"What's going on?" Matt asked as nearly everyone came into the room where he was sitting up in the bed with his leg propped up.

"I have a surprise for you," Jessica said, holding out a pair of crutches.

Matt tilted his head. "Crutches?"

She laughed, the sound light and airy. "No. You need to use the crutches to come see your surprise."

His eyes narrowed. "You just want me to get my lazy butt out of bed."

Jessica's smile grew. "Yep. That's it. You've been laying around long enough. We have a lot of work to do."

He moved to the edge of the bed and took the crutches, then slowly stood.

"Take your time," Jessica said, an edge of concern to her voice.

"Oh," Matt laughed, "now you're worried about me."

"Come on," Jeff said with a grin, "we don't have all day."

Everyone backed out of the room, giving Matt plenty of

space to hobble out. "Where's this surprise?" he asked, looking around the family room.

Jessica opened the front door and stepped onto the porch. "Come outside."

Derrick enjoyed watching the perplexed expression on Matt's face—he had no idea what they'd brought back from their battle with the Emperors.

Finally, Matt made it onto the porch. Jessica swept her hand outward to encompass the truck and RV parked in the driveway.

Matt's mouth fell open and his eyebrows shot up as a sound of surprise left his mouth. He looked at Jessica with incredulity. "Is that ours?"

Derrick had never seen her smile so brightly.

"Yes," she said. "We got it back."

"But...how?"

Matt's reaction was better than Derrick had expected. He laughed. "We found it at the Emperors' headquarters."

Matt turned to Derrick, his expression sober. "Wish I could have been there."

Smiling, Derrick patted him on the back. "I know. Good news is, once your leg's healed, there will be plenty of work for you to do."

Matt laughed. "Looking forward to it."

"Come take a look inside," Jessica said.

At Matt's look of hesitation, Derrick said, "Don't worry. She cleaned out all traces of that loser."

With help from Derrick and Chris, Matt made his way

down the porch steps and went to the open door of the RV. Again with help, he climbed up the steps and inside. "What? You found the seeds!"

Derrick chuckled. Randy hadn't bothered to remove the packets of seeds that Jessica had stored in a cabinet, and when she'd found them, she'd laid them out on the counter to show Matt.

Derrick stepped out of the RV to let Matt and Jessica celebrate. He joined the others who were standing nearby.

At lunch, the entire group—except those on watch—gathered on the covered patio to celebrate their successes. Things were looking up. Seeing the happy and relaxed faces made winning the battle against the Emperors all the sweeter for Derrick.

"Today we're having a feast," Sarah said as she, Kayla, and Brooke carried trays of food out of the house, setting them on the serving table.

As the incredible scent of freshly baked bread hit him, Derrick felt his stomach rumble.

Halfway through the meal, Chris, who was on watch, appeared with Walter right behind him.

Frank stood and embraced his friend. "Join us."

Smiling, Walter said, "Don't mind if I do, but first I want to thank every one of you for what you did for my grandkids last night." His eyes shone with unshed tears. "You have no idea how happy we are to have them back."

"How are they doing?" Jessica asked.

He inhaled deeply and slowly exhaled. "As well as can be expected. But the important thing is that they're home."

"What about those two women?" Chris asked. "Did they make it home okay?"

Walter smiled brightly. "Yes. Scott and Charlie took them home. You can imagine how happy their families were to see them again."

Derrick wondered what Walter's grandkids and the two women had gone through but decided he didn't want to know the details. He and his people had done their part ridding the world of the blight of the Emperors. Now they could focus on truly settling in to their new reality and adjusting the way they lived to make it not only survivable, but enjoyable.

Walter frowned. "I didn't only come here to thank you. I came here to warn you as well."

CHAPTER TWENTY-SEVEN

Derrick

"Warn us?" Frank asked. "About what?"

Walter pulled a bright yellow sheet of paper out of his back pocket and handed it to Frank, who held it up and began reading. "For the safety of all citizens, a mandatory gun buyback has been instituted by the state of California. Effective immediately."

Derrick's eyes went wide as his heart thudded in his chest. "What?"

Frank looked his way. "Says here to bring all of our weapons to an address and they'll pay us with food, water, and other critical supplies."

Derrick couldn't believe this. "Guns *are* critical supplies."

Nodding, Frank said, "Couldn't agree more."

Derrick tried to imagine what it would have been like to go up against the fully armed Emperors with nothing but knives and fists. He sighed and shook his head. "I'm sure people like Randy would turn all of their guns right over to the government. Then we'll all be safe."

Jeff leaned forward, his expression intense. "That's what some people actually believe. Take all the guns from the law-abiding citizens and then there will be no more guns." He shook his head and muttered, "Idiots."

"Mandatory buyback sounds like a polite way to say gun confiscation," Matt said.

Heads nodded all around.

"Does it say what they'll do if people refuse?" Chris asked.

Frank scanned the page. "Nope. Just says there's a short grace period for cooperation."

Derrick didn't like the sound of that. "Meaning, when that unknown time period is over, all bets are off."

Jeff leaned back in his chair. "Far as I'm concerned, they can all go straight to hell. They'll have to pry my gun from my cold, dead fingers."

Derrick silently nodded.

"How can they enforce this?" Emily asked.

Shrugging, Jeff said, "No idea. But remember those guys who came by a week ago? Said they were from the government? Claimed to be taking a census? Now that they've been here they have to have a pretty good idea how many weapons we have." He shook his head. "Don't be surprised if they show up again. On a different mission."

Derrick turned to Walter. "Did they come by your place?"

Grimacing, Walter nodded. "Yeah. I didn't like the way

they made themselves at home. Wandering off and poking through my property."

"Those guys are almost as bad as the Emperors," Frank said, his expression fierce. "They held a gun to my Sarah to disarm us."

Derrick had heard about that but hadn't witnessed it. He couldn't begin to imagine how upset Frank had been.

"I'm fine, sweetheart," Sarah said as she put a hand on Frank's arm.

Frank scowled at the ground and shook his head, obviously still deeply upset by the whole experience.

Derrick, on the other hand, worried about what might happen next. They had enough on their shoulders just trying to survive without the government putting its heavy boot on their necks. "We need to be prepared."

"What should we do?" Emily asked.

Derrick looked her way. "We already have the road blocked off and camouflaged, but they've been here once. I'm sure they'll be able to find it again. No doubt they took notes on everything about this place." He paused. "To be fair to all of you, you need to decide if you want to cooperate with this buyback. It says there's a grace period for cooperation." He looked at each person in turn. Everyone's eyes flashed the same anger he felt. "Does anyone want to participate?"

"No way," Chris said, nearly spitting the words out.

The others nodded their agreement, saying, "Forget it," and "uh-uh," and "Hell no."

Smiling grimly, Derrick nodded. "Okay. We're all on the

same page. Good. Because if the government is serious about this, and after what happened at the border on our way here I'm certain they are, we're going to have to deal with them eventually. You can count on it."

"We need to find out more about the person in charge," Matt said. He shifted his eyes to Frank and Walter. "Do you know who the Governor is?"

"Last I heard," Frank said, "it was Shane Moffit." He looked to Walter.

Walter nodded. "Yeah. I think that's who's in charge. He was the State Treasurer before everyone above him died from the bird flu."

Derrick wondered how many people were working for Governor Moffit and how many of them believed in this mandatory buyback. He was certain there were plenty who supported the idea, but there had to be some in the government who disagreed.

The world was filled with desperate, evil people. But there were plenty of good people too. Like Walter and Jack and the others in their group. If they could find good people to be on their side, they could fight this government overreach and triumph once again.

Then Derrick thought about Ben. They'd been lucky to only lose one person in that battle. Going up against the government would be a whole different thing. They'd need time to recon and plan. Time he wasn't sure they had. Even so, what choice did they have? They couldn't turn over their guns. How would they protect themselves against thieves and murderers if they were unarmed? Not to mention protecting themselves against the tyranny of the government, tyranny which seemed to be happening right before their eyes.

"What are you thinking about, Derrick?" Matt asked.

He lifted his gaze. All eyes were on him. They were looking to him for leadership once again. And once again, he would rise to the challenge. He sat up straight and set his jaw. "We have a lot of work to do."

———

Thank you for reading No Safe Place! The final book in the series, Insurrection, is available now.

ABOUT THE AUTHOR

Christine has always loved to read, but enjoys writing suspenseful novels as well. She has her own eReader and is not embarrassed to admit that she is a book hoarder. One of Christine's favorite activities is to go camping with her family and read, read, read while enjoying the beauty of nature.

I love to hear from my readers. You can contact me in any of the following ways:
www.christinekersey.com
christine@christinekersey.com

Made in the USA
Coppell, TX
08 February 2022